Harry Harrison was born in Stamford, Connecticut, grew up in New York City and, promptly on his eighteenth birthday, was drafted into the United States Army. Returning to civilian life some years later, he pursued careers as an artist, art director and editor until, one day, he found himself following a new occupation as free-lance writer. Since then he has lived with his family in more than twenty-seven countries including Mexico, England, Italy and Denmark. The Harrisons now live in Ireland.

By the same author

*Deathworld 1*
*Deathworld 2*
*Deathworld 3*
*The Stainless Steel Rat*
*The Stainless Steel Rat's Revenge*
*The Stainless Steel Rat Saves the World*
*The Stainless Steel Rat Wants You!*
*The Stainless Steel Rat for President*
*Bill, the Galactic Hero*
*The Technicolor Time Machine*
*Make Room! Make Room!*
*Star Smashers of the Galaxy Rangers*
*The California Iceberg*
*Planet of the Damned*
*Plague from Space*
*The Men from P.I.G. and R.O.B.O.T.*
*In Our Hands, The Stars*
*Spaceship Medic*
*A Transatlantic Tunnel, Hurrah!*
*One Step from Earth*
*Prime Number*
*Montezuma's Revenge*
*Queen Victoria's Revenge*
*Skyfall*
*Two Tales and Eight Tomorrows*
*War with the Robots*
*The Best of Harry Harrison*
*Backdrop of Stars*
*Planet Story* (illustrated)
*Great Balls of Fire* (non-fiction)
*Mechanismo* (non-fiction)
*Spacecraft in Fact and Fiction* (with Malcolm Edwards)
    (non-fiction)
*Homeworld*
*Wheelworld*
*The QE2 is Missing*
*Stonehenge* (with Leon E. Stover)
*Rebel in Time*

# HARRY HARRISON

# Starworld

Volume 3 in the *To the Stars* trilogy

This first hardcover edition published in Great Britain 1988 by
SEVERN HOUSE PUBLISHERS LTD of
40–42 William IV Street, London WC2N 4DF

British Library Cataloguing in Publication Data
Harrison, Harry, *1925–*
Starworld
I. Title
813'.54 [F]
ISBN 0–7278–1632–9

Printed and bound in Great Britain

# Chapter One

The battered freighter had been on fusion drive ever since it had passed the orbit of Mars. It was pointed at Earth – or rather at the place where the Earth would be in a few hours' time. All of its electronic apparatus had been either shut down or was operating at the absolute minimum output – behind heavy shielding. The closer they came to Earth the greater their chance of detection. And their instant destruction.

'We're taking the war to them,' the political commander said. Before the revolution he had been a professor of economics at a small university on a distant planet; the emergency had changed everything.

'You don't have to convince me,' Blakeney said. 'I was on the committee that ordered this attack. And I'm not happy with the discrimination target program.'

'I'm not trying to convince. I'm just enjoying the thought. I had family on Teoranta . . . '

'They're gone,' Blakeney said. 'The planet's gone. You have to forget them.'

'No. I want to remember them. As far as I am concerned this attack is being launched in their memory. And in memory of all the others savaged and destroyed by Earth down through the centuries. We're fighting back at last. Taking the war to them.'

'I'm still concerned about the software.'

'You worry too much. One single bomb has to be dropped on Australia. How can you miss an island that big, an entire continent?'

'I'll tell you exactly how. When we release the

scoutship it will have our velocity and will accelerate from that basic speed. The computer cannot make a mistake because there will be time for only a single pass. Do you realize what the closing velocity will be? Tremendous!' He took out his calculator and began punching in figures. The ship's commander raised his hand.

'Enough. I have no head for mathematics. I know only that our best people modified the scoutship for this attack. The DNA constructed virus will eat and destroy any food crop. You yourself prepared the program to pilot the ship, to locate the target, to drop the bomb. They'll know it's war then.'

'It's because I worked on the program that I am unsure. Too many variables. I'm going down for another test run.'

'Do that. I'm perfectly secure, but please yourself. But watch the time. Only a few hours more. Once we penetrate their detection net it will have to be hit and run with no staying around to watch the results.'

'It won't take long,' Blakeney said, turning and leaving the bridge.

Everything has been jury-rigged, he thought as he went down the empty corridors of the ship. Even the crew. An unarmed freighter daring to attack the heart of the Earth Commonwealth. But the plan was wild enough to work. They had been building up speed ever since they had shut down the space drive, well outside the orbit of Mars. The ship should hurtle past Earth and be safely away before the defenders could launch a counter-attack. But as they passed the planet the small scoutship they carried, secured to the outer hull, would be launched under computer control. This was what worried him. All the circuitry was breadboarded, lashed together, a complicated oneshot. If it failed the entire mission failed. He

6

would have to go through all of the tests just one last time.

The tiny spacecraft, smaller even than a normal lifeboat, was secured to the outer hull by steel braces equipped with explosive bolts. A crawl tube had been fixed in place so that the scoutship shared the larger ship's atmosphere, making installation and servicing that much easier. Blakeney slipped in through the tube, then frowned at the circuits and apparatus bolted onto the walls of the tiny cabin. He turned on the screen, punched up the inspection menu and began running through the tests.

On the bridge an alarm sounded hoarsely and a series of numbers began marching across the watch operator's screen. The political commander came and looked over his shoulder.

'What does it mean?' he asked.

'We've crossed their detection web, probably the outermost one from Earth.'

'Then they know that we're here?'

'Not necessarily. We're on the plane of the ecliptic...'

'Translation?'

'The imaginary plane, the level on which all of the planets in the solar system ride. Also all of the meteoric debris. We're too far out for them to have caught any radiation from the ship so we're just another hunk of space junk, a ferrous meteor. Now. The web's alerted to us and more apparatus will be trained in our direction. Laser, radar, whatever they have. At least it should work like that. We'll find out soon. We're recording all their signals. When we get back we'll have a record of everything. When it's analysed we'll know a good deal more about how their set-up works.'

*When,* the political commander thought, not *if.* Nothing wrong with the morale. But there was another half to

7

this mission. The virus strike. He looked at the time readout and called through to the scoutship.

'We're entering the red zone now. Less than half an hour to separation. How are you doing?'

'Just finishing up. As soon as I clear this program I'll join you.'

'Good. I want you to ... '

'Pulsed radar locked onto us!' the watch operator called out. 'They know we're here.' An auxiliary screen lit up near his elbow and he pointed to the readout. 'Our reflectors have been launched. So where they had one blip on their screens before they now have a half dozen all the same, but separating at different speeds on different courses.'

'They won't know which one is the real ship?'

'Not at the moment. But they know what we've done and they'll start analyzing course predictions, forwards and back in time. They'll spot the real one. But by the time their computers have worked that out, ours will have initiated other defences. It's a good program. Written by the best physicists and comptechs.'

The political commander was less than reassured by the operator's reasoning. He did not like to think that his life depended on the non-random dispersal of magnetic charges and electrons that made up the program. Playing an intellectual game with the enemy computers. He looked out at the tiny sparks of the stars, the growing disc of the Earth, and tried to imagine the web of light beams and radio waves surging around them. He could not. He had to take it on faith that they were there and working at speeds infinitely beyond his own. A human being could not fight a battle in space. The machines did that. The crew were just captive spectators. His hands were clenched tightly behind his back, though he was not aware of it.

There was a series of small thudding sounds, more felt than heard, followed by an explosion that actually shook the deck beneath his feet.

'We've been hit!' he called out unthinkingly.

'Not yet.' The watch operator glanced at his screens. 'All of our remaining dupes and reflectors have been launched, then the scoutship. Mission accomplished – but now we have to get out of here. Fusion drive cut . . . space drive circuits now energized. As soon as the gravity fields allow we'll be on our way.'

The political commander's eyes widened at a sudden thought; he turned sharply about.

'Where's Blakeney?' he called out. But no one on the bridge had heard him. They were counting the seconds, waiting for the missiles that must have surely been launched in their direction.

The political commander felt a sudden arrow of despair. He knew where Blakeney was.

He had been right, absolutely right! And they called themselves comptechs. They couldn't write a program to win at tic-tac-toe. Orbital mechanics, fine, simple trig and geometry and calculus. Child's play. But comparison plane orientation was apparently well beyond them.

Blakeney watched with satisfaction for less than a second while the cursor on the computer roved all over the highly amplified image of Earth – then froze on the great sweep of a circular storm over Europe. He switched on the override and put his finger on the screen, on the only bit of Australia clear of the cloud cover of a tropical storm. When the glowing blob of the cursor jumped to this spot he typed in POSITIVE IDENTIFICATION and took his finger away. At least the moronic thing could be counted upon to stay there once orientated.

None to early. The engine note changed as the course

shifted, just moments later. Good. He followed the program display, then unlocked the launching switch as they hurtled towards the top of the atmosphere, ready to release manually if there were any more difficulties.

There were none. At the same instant that zero appeared on the screen the ejection mechanism thudded heavily. As the ship arced slowly away to avoid the outer traces of atmosphere, the heavy ceramic container was hurtling towards Earth. He knew what would be happening next; this thing at least had been well designed. Layer after layer of ablative material would burn away as it impacted on the thickening air. It would grow hot – and slow down – with the frozen virus locked safely into the cryogenic flask inside. Then a layer of ceramic would fall away to reveal an opening for the air to enter, to impact on a pressure gauge inside.

At exactly 10,769 metres, in the middle of the jet stream, the explosive charge would explode releasing the contents of the flask.

The wind would carry the virus across Australia, perhaps to New Zealand as well. A carefully designed virus that would attack and destroy any and all of the food crops grown on Earth.

Blakeney smiled at the thought as the missile hit.

It had an atomic warhead so that, to the watchers below, there was suddenly a new sun just visible through the clouds.

# Chapter Two

The TWA jet had left New York a few hours after dark. As soon as it had reached its cruising altitude it had gone supersonic and cut a booming path straight across the United States. About the time it was crossing Kansas the western sky had grown light as the Mach 2.5 craft caught up with the setting sun. The sun was well above the horizon again when they lost altitude over Arizona, and the passengers who had seen one sunset in New York City now witnessed a far more colourful one over the Mojave desert.

Thurgood-Smythe squinted into the glare then opaqued his window. He was going through the notes of the emergency meeting that had been hurriedly called at the UN and had no eyes either for the glories of the sunset or the massed technology of Spaceconcent opening up before him. His attaché case rested on his knees with the flat VDU screen pulled out of its slot. The figures, names, dates marched steadily across the screen, stopping only when he touched the keyboard to correct any transcription errors made by the speech recorder. It had been programmed for his voice, but still substituted *one* for *won* a good deal of the time. He made the corrections automatically, still taken aback by the momentous changes and the immense gravity of the situation. What had happened was unbelievable, impossible. But happened it had.

There was a jar as they touched down, then he was thrust forward against the safety harness as the engines reversed. The screen and keyboard disappeared at the touch of a button; the dark window cleared and he looked out at the white towers of the space center, now washed with glowing ochre by the sun. He was the first passenger off the plane.

Two uniformed guards were waiting for him; he nodded at their snapped salutes. Nothing was said, nor did they ask for his identification. They knew who he was, knew also that this was an unscheduled flight arranged for his benefit. Thurgood-Smythe's beak-like nose and lean, hard features had been made familiar by the news reports. His short-cropped white hair appeared severely military compared to the longer haired styles currently in fashion. He looked exactly what he was; someone in charge.

Auguste Blanc was standing at the ceiling-high window, his back turned, when Thurgood-Smythe came in. As Director of Spaceconcent his office was naturally on the top floor of the tallest administration building. The view was impressive; the sunset incomparable. The mountains on the horizon were purple-black, outlined against the red of the sky. All of the buildings and the towering spaceships were washed by the same fiery color. The colour of blood; prophetic perhaps. Nonsense! A cough cut through Auguste Blanc's thoughts and he turned to face Thurgood-Smythe.

'A good flight, I sincerely hope,' he said, extending his hand. A thin, delicate hand, as finally drawn as his features. He had a title, a very good French one, but he rarely used it. The people he needed to impress, such as Thurgood-Smythe, took no heed of such things. Thurgood-Smythe nodded sharply, impatient for the formalities to be out of the way.

'But tiring nevertheless. A restorative, then? Something to drink, to relax?'

'No thank you, Auguste. No, wait, a Perrier. If you please.'

12

'The dry air of the airship. Not humidified as we of course have in the spacers. Here you are.' He passed over the tall glass, then poured an Armagnac for himself. Without turning about, as though ashamed of what he was saying, he spoke into the bottles of the cocktail cabinet. 'Is it bad? As bad as I have heard?'

'I don't know what you have heard.'

Thurgood-Smythe took a long drink from his glass. 'But I can tell you this, in all secrecy . . . '

'This room is secure.'

' . . . it is far worse than any of us thought. A débâcle.' He dropped into an armchair and stared sightlessly into his glass. 'We've lost. Everywhere. Not a single planet remains within our control –'

'That cannot be!' The sophistication was gone and there was an edge of animal fear in Auguste Blanc's voice. 'Our deepspace bases, how could they be taken?'

'I'm not talking about those. They're unimportant. All of them on low gravity, airless moons. They aren't self-sufficient, they must be supplied regularly. More of a handicap than an asset. They can't be attacked – but they can be starved out. We're evacuating them all.'

'You cannot! They are our foothold, the cutting edge of the blade for conquest . . . '

'They are our Achilles heel, if you wish to continue this stupid simile.' There was no trace of politeness, no touch of warmth in Thurgood-Smythe's voice now. 'We need the transport and we need the men. Here is an order. See that it goes out on the Foscolo net at once.' He took a single sheet of paper from his case and passed it over to the trembling director. 'The debate is done. Two days of it. This is the combined decision.'

Auguste Blanc's hands were shaking in the most craven manner so that he had difficulty reading the paper he grasped. But the director was needed. He was good at his

13

job. For this reason, and none other, Thurgood-Smythe spoke quietly, considerately.

'These decision's are sometimes harder to make than to implement. I'm sorry, Auguste. They left us no choice. The planets are theirs. All of them: They planned well. Our people are captured or dead. We have most of our space fleet intact, there was no way they could get at them, though a few were sabotaged, a few deserted. We're pulling back. A strategic withdrawal. A regrouping.'

'Retreat.' He spoke bitterly. 'Then we have lost already.'

'No. Not in the slightest. We have the spacers, and among them are the only ships designed for military use. The enemy have freighters, tugs, a handful of deserters. Many of their worlds already face starvation. While they are thinking about survival we shall reinforce our defences. When they try to attack us they will certainly be defeated. Then, one by one, we will reoccupy. You and I will probably not see the end, not in our time, but this rebellion will eventually be stifled and crushed. That is what will be done.'

'What must I do?' Auguste Blanc asked, still insecure.

'Send this command. It is a security order to all commanders to change codes. I am sure that the old one is compromised by now.'

Auguste Blanc looked at the incomprehensible series of letters and numbers, then nodded. Encoding and decoding were a computer function and he neither knew nor cared how they operated. He slid the sheet into the reader slot in his desk top and tapped a series of commands on the keyboard. A few seconds after he had done this the response sounded from the computer speakers.

'Command issued to all receivers listed. Response

received from all receivers listed. Communication code has been changed.'

Thurgood-Smythe nodded when he heard this and put another sheet of paper onto Auguste Blanc's desk.

'You will notice that the orders are issued in very general terms. The fleet to be withdrawn to Earth orbit as soon as possible, all advanced bases to be deactivated, the Lunar bases to be reinforced. As soon as enough transports are available they will be used to ferry troops to the Earth orbiting colonies. They will be occupied in force. I have positive information that the colonies' sympathies are with the rebels, not with their home world. And the same thing will be done with the orbital satellite stations. Do you have any questions?'

'Will there be a shortage of food? I heard that we are going to go hungry. I had my wife send in a large order for food but it was not filled. What does it mean?'

The man is a coward – and a fool, Thurgood-Smythe thought to himself. Worried about his failure to be a hoarder! I suppose that is a new word to him. And to most people. They'll find out what it means when we shoot a few of them. For hoarding and spreading defeatist rumours as well.

'I'll tell you the truth,' Thurgood-Smythe said aloud, 'but I'm going to give you a warning first. We are in a war, and morale is very important in wartime. So people who spread false rumours, who attempt to hoard food depriving others of their share – these people are aiding the enemy and they will be punished. Punishment will be imprisonment and execution. Am I expressing myself clearly enough for you?'

'Yes, I didn't really understand. I really am sorry, had no idea . . .'

The man was trembling again; Thurgood-Smythe tried not to let his distaste show in his expression. 'Very good.

There will be no starvation on Earth – but there will be shortages and rationing. We have always imported a certain amount of prole food, but I don't think either of us will worry if their rations are short. More important is the fact that a blight has destroyed all of the Australian food crops for this growing season ... '

'Blight? All their crops ... I don't understand.'

'Mutated virus. Spread by bombing from space. Self-eliminating after a few months but it will mean completly replanting all of the food crops with imported seed.'

'You must destroy them all! Criminal rebels – they are trying to starve us to death!'

'Not really. They were just delivering a warning. It appears that in enthusiasm for revenge some of our space commanders took individual actions. At least two rebel planets have been effectively destroyed. The rebel reaction was to send this ship to bomb Australia. It could just as easily have decimated the entire world's food crops. It was a message. We of course took out the attacking ship. But we have sent a return message agreeing to their terms. Planetary bombings only of military targets.'

'We must wipe them out, every single one of them,' Auguste Blanc said, hoarsely.

'We will. Our plan is a simple one. Withdraw all our forces to Earth orbit to secure against any invasion or occupation of the space colonies and satellites. Then selective reconquest of the planets, one by one. All of our spacers are being fitted with weapons. The enemy have only a few ships manned by traitors. They may have won these battles. We will win the war ... '

'Urgent report,' the computer said. A sheet of paper emerged from the desk top. Auguste Blanc looked at it then passed it over.

'It is addressed to you,' he said.

Thurgood-Smythe read it quickly; then smiled.

'I ordered all reports of enemy ship movements to be screened and analysed. They need food more than we do. They have now sent a number of ships to Halvmörk. One of the largest food planets. I want those ships to land and load completely. Then leave ...'

'So we can capture them!' Auguste Blanc was exuberant, his earlier fears forgotten for the moment. 'A genius of a plan, Thurgood-Smythe, may I congratulate you. They brought this war upon themselves and now they will pay. We will take the food and give them starvation in return.'

'Exactly what I had in mind, Auguste. Exactly.'

They smiled at each other with sadistic pleasure.

'They have only themselves to blame,' Thurgood-Smythe said. 'We gave them peace and they gave us war. We will now show them the high price that must be paid for that decision. When we are done with them there will be peace in the galaxy forever. They have forgotten that they are the children of Earth, that we built the commonwealth of planets for their sakes. They have forgotten what it cost to terraform all of their planets to make them suitable for occupation by mankind, the cost in lives and money. They have rebelled against our gentle hand of rule. We shall now clench this hand into a fist and they shall be punished. They started this rebellion, this war – but we will finish it.'

# Chapter Three

'You're going now,' Alzbeta said. She spoke calmly, almost emotionlessly, but her hands were clenched hard on Jan's. They stood in the shadow of a great bulk grain carrier, one of the shining cylinders of metal that rose up high behind them. He looked down into her gentle features and could find no words to answer with; he simply nodded. The love in her face, the yearning there, they were too much for him and he had to turn away.

It was the irony of life that after all his lonely years on this twilight planet, now, married and a father to be, with a measure of peace and happiness at last, now was the time he had to leave. But there were no alternatives. He was the only one here who would fight for the rights of the people of this agricultural world, who might possibly see to it that some day a complete and decent society might grow on this planet. Because he was the only one on Halvmörk who had been born on Earth and who knew the realities of existence there and in the rest of the Earth Commonwealth. Halvmörk was a dead-end world now, where the inhabitants were agricultural slaves, working to feed the other planets for no return other than their bare existence. In the present emergency the rebel planets would expect them to keep on working as they always had. Well they would farm still – but only if they could be free of their planetary prison. Free to be part of the Commonwealth culture, free to have their children educated – and finally free to change the artificial and stunted society forced upon them by Earth. Jan knew he would not be thanked, or even liked, for what he was going to do. He would do it still. He owed it to the generations to come. To his own child among others.

'The orbits have been calculated. We will have to lift the ships very soon,' he said.

Alzbeta looked steadfastedly into Jan Kulozik's face as he spoke, memorizing those thin, taut features. She put her arms about his wiry and hard-muscled body then, pressing tight against it, so that the child within her was between them, in the sheltered warmth of their bodies, clutching hard as though when she released him she might never hold him again. It was a possibility she did not consider, yet it was lurking just out of sight all of the time. There was a war being fought among the alien stars and he was going to it. But he would come back; that was the only thought she would let her brain hold on to.

'Come back to me,' she whispered aloud, then pulled away from him, running towards their home. Not wanting to look at him again, afraid that she would break down and make him ashamed.

'Ten minutes,' Debhu called out from the foot of the boarding ladder. 'Let's get aboard and strap in.'

Jan turned and climbed up the ladder. One of the crewmen was waiting in the airlock and he sealed the outer hatch as soon as they had passed through.

'I'm going to the bridge,' Debhu said. 'Since you've never been in space you'll strap in on deck . . . '

'I've worked in free fall,' Jan said.

The question was on Debhu's lips, but he never spoke it. Halvmörk was a prison planet. It no longer mattered any longer why anyone should have been sent here. 'Good,' he finally said. 'I can use you. We have lost a lot of trained men. Most of the crew have never been in space before. Come with me to the bridge.'

Jan found the operation a fascinating one. He must have arrived on Halvmörk in a ship very much like this one –

but he had no memory of it. All he remembered was a windowless prison cell on a spacer. And drugged food that kept him docile and easily controlled. Then unconsciousness, to waken to find the ships gone and himself a castaway. It had all happened far too many years ago.

But this was very different. The ship they were aboard was identified only by a number, as were all of the other tugs. It was a brute, built for power alone, capable of lifting a thousand times its own mass. Like the other tugs it lived in space, in perpetual orbit. To be used only once every four Earth years when the seasons changed on this twilight planet. Then, before the fields burned in summer and the inhabitants moved to the new winter hemisphere, the ships would come for their crops. Deep spacers, spider-like vessels that were built in space for space, that could never enter a planet's atmosphere. They would emerge from space drive and go into orbit about the planet, only then unlocking from the great tubes of the bulk carriers they had brought. Then it would be the time to use the tugs.

When the crews changed over the dormant, orbiting ships would glow with life, light and warmth as their power would be turned on, their stored air released and warmed. They in their turn would lock to the empty bulk carriers and carefully pull them from orbit, killing their velocity until they dropped into the atmosphere below, easing them gently down to the surface.

The carriers were loaded now, with food to feed the hungry rebel planets. Their blasting ascent was smooth, computer controlled, perfect. Rising up, faster and faster through the atmosphere, out of the atmosphere, into the eternal blinding sunlight of space. The computer program that controlled this operation had been written by comptechs now centuries dead. Their work lived after them. Radar determined proximity. Orbits were matched, gas

20

jets flared, great bulks of metal weighing thousands of tonnes drifted slowly together with micrometric precision. They closed, touched, engaged, sealed one to the other.

'All connections completed,' the computer said, while displaying the same information on the screen. 'Ready to unlock and transfer crew.'

Debhu activated the next phase of the program. One after another the gigantic grapples disengaged, sending shudders of sound through the tug's frame. Once free of its mighty burden the tug drifted away, then jetted towards the deep spacer that was now lashed to the cargo of grain. Gentle contact was made and the airlock of one ship was sealed to the other. As soon as the connection was complete the inner door opened automatically.

'Let's transfer,' Debhu said, leading the way. 'We usually remain while the tugs put themselves into orbit and power down to standby status. Not this time. When each ship is secure it is cleared to depart. Every one of them has a different destination. This food is vitally needed.'

A low buzzer was sounding on the bridge and one of the readouts was flashing red. 'Not too serious,' Debhu said. 'It's a grapple lock, not secured. Could be a monitoring failure or dirt in the jaws. They pick it up when we drop planetside. Do you want to take a look at it?'

'No problem,' Jan said. 'That's the kind of work I have been doing ever since I came to this planet. Where are the suits?'

The tool kit was an integral part of the suit, as was the computer radio link that would direct him to the malfunctioning unit where the trouble was. The suit rustled and expanded as the air was pumped from the lock; then the outer hatch swung open.

Jan had no time to appreciate the glory of the stars, unshielded now by any planetary atmosphere. Their journey could not begin until he had done his work. He activated the direction finder, then pulled himself along the handbar in the direction indicated by the holographic green arrow that apparently floated in space before him. Then stopped abruptly as a column of ice particles suddenly sprang out of the hull at his side. Other growing pillars came into being all around him; he smiled to himself and pushed on. The ship was venting the air from the cargo. The air and water vapour froze instantly into tiny ice particles as it emerged. The vacuum of space would dehydrate and preserve the corn, lightening the cargo and helping to prevent the interplanetary spread of organisms.

The frozen plumes were dying down and drifting away by the time he came to the grapple. He used the key to open the cover of the control box and activated the manual override. Motors whirred, he could feel their vibration through the palm of his hand, and the massive jaws slowly ground apart. He looked closely at their smooth surfaces, at what appeared to be a ice-crystalled clump of mud flattened on one of them. He brushed it away and pressed the switch in the control box. This time the jaws closed all the way and a satisfactory green light appeared. Not the world's most difficult repair he thought as he sealed the box again.

'Return at once!' the radio squawked loudly in his ears, then went dead. No explanation given. He unclipped his safety line and began to pull back in the direction of the airlock.

It was closed. Locked. Sealed.

While he was still assimilating this incredible fact, trying to get a response on his radio, he saw the reason.

Another deep spacer came drifting across their bow, reaction jets flaring, magnetic grapples hurling towards them, trailing their cables. Clearly visible on its side in the harsh sunlight was a familiar blue globe on white.

The flag of Earth.

For long seconds Jan just hung there, the sound of his heart pounding heavy in his ears, trying to understand what was happening. It suddenly became obvious when he saw the spacelock on the other ship begin to open.

Of course. The Earth forces weren't going to give up that easily. They were out there, watching. They had observed the food convoy being assembled, had easily guessed the destination. And Earth needed the food in these hulls just as much as the rebel planets did. Needed it to eat – and as a weapon to starve their opponents into submission. They could not have it!

Jan's anger flared just as the first of the suited figures emerged and dropped towards the hull close to him. They must be stopped. He groped through his tool kit, pulled out the largest powered screwdriver there and thumbed it on, full speed. It whined to life, its integral counterweight spinning to neutralize the twisting action on his body. He held this extemporized weapon before him as he launched himself at the approaching spacemen.

Surprise was on his side; he had not been seen in the shadows on the spacer's skin. The man half-turned as Jan came up, but he was too late. Jan pushed the whirling blade against the other's side, clutched onto him so he would not drift away, watched the metal bite into the tough fabric – then saw the plume of frozen air jet out. The man arched, struggled – then went limp. Jan pushed the corpse away, turned, kicked to one side so the man coming towards him floated harmlessly by. He was ready then to jab his weapon at another spaceman coming along behind him.

It was not as easy to do the second time. The man struggled as Jan clutched his arm. They tumbled about, floating and twisting, until someone grabbed Jan by the leg. Then still another.

It was an unequal struggle and he could not win. They were armed, he saw rocket guns ready in their hands, but they holstered them as they held him. Jan stopped struggling. They were not going to kill him – for the moment. They obviously wanted prisoners. He was overwhelmed by a sense of blackest despair as they pulled him to one side as more attackers poured by, then dragged him back into their ship and through the spacelock. Once it was sealed they stripped the spacesuit from him and hurled him to the floor. One of them stepped forward and kicked him hard against the side of the head, then over and over again in the ribs until the pain blacked out his vision. They wanted their prisoners alive, but not necessarily unbruised. That was the last thing he remembered as the boot caught him in the head again and he roared down into pain-filled darkness.

# Chapter Four

'Some they killed,' Debhu said, holding the wet cloth to the side of Jan's head, 'but only if they fought too hard and it was dangerous to capture them. They wanted prisoners. The rest of us were outnumbered, clubbed down. Does that feel any better.'

'Feels like my skull is crumbling inside.'

'No, it's just bruising. They've sewn up the cuts. No broken ribs, the doctor said. They want us in good shape for public display when we get to Earth. They can't have taken many prisoners before they captured us. It hasn't been that kind of a war.' He hesitated a second, then spoke more quietly. 'Do you have a record? I mean, is there any reason they would like to know who you were, to identify you?'

'Why do you want to know?'

'I've never been to Earth, or in direct contact with Earthies before. They may have records on me, I can't be sure. But they took retinal photographs of us all. You too, while you were unconscious.'

Jan nodded, then closed his eyes briefly at the pain that followed the movement.

'I think they will be very happy when they identify me,' he said. 'I doubt if I will be.'

The pattern made by the small blood vessels inside the eye is far more individual than any fingerprint. It can be neither forged nor altered. Everyone on Earth had this pattern recorded at birth and at regular intervals thereafter. Given a retinal print a computer could sort through these billions of photographs in a few moments. They would come up with his. Along with his identity and his criminal record. They would be very glad to discover these interesting facts.

'Not that it's worth worrying about anyway,' Debhu said, leaning back against the metal wall of their prison. 'We're all for the knackers in any case. Probably a show trial first to entertain the proles. Then – who knows what. Nothing good I'm sure. An easy death is the best we can hope for.'

'No it's not,' Jan said, ignoring the pain, forcing himself to sit up. 'We are going to have to escape.'

Debhu smiled sympthetically. 'Yes. I suppose we ought to.'

'Don't patronize me,' Jan said angrily. 'I know what I'm saying. I'm from Earth, which is more than anyone else in this room can say. I know how these people think and work. We're dead anyway so we have nothing to lose by trying.'

'If we break out of here we have no way of taking over the ship. Not from armed men.'

'That's the answer then. We don't do a thing now. We wait until we've landed. There will be guards of course, but the rest of the crew will be at their stations. We won't have to take over the ship. Just get away from it.'

'Simple enough.' Debhu smiled. 'I'm with you so far. Now do you have any suggestions how we get out of this locked cell?'

'Plenty. I want you to move around quietly among the others. I want everything they have. Watches, tools, coins, anything. Whatever they were left with. When I see what they have I'll tell you how we are going to get out of here.'

Jan did not want to explain, to give them any false hopes. He rested and drank some water, looking around the bare metal room in which they had been imprisoned.

26

There were some thin mattresses scattered about on the hard plastic floor, a sink and toilet unit secured to one wall. A single, barred door was set into the opposite wall. No spying devices were visible, but that did not necessarily mean that they weren't there. He would take what precautions he could, hoping that their captors' surveillance would be a casual one.

'How do they feed us?' Jan asked as Debhu dropped down beside him.

'They pass the food through that slide in the door. Thin disposable dishes, like that cup you have there. Nothing we can use for weapons.'

'I wasn't thinking of that. What's beyond the door?'

'Short length of hall. Then another locked door. Both doors are never opened at the same time.'

'Better and better. Is there a guard in that short stretch of hall?'

'Not that I've ever seen. No need for it. We've got some things for you from the men . . . '

'Don't show me yet. Just tell me.'

'Junk for the most part. Coins, keys, a nail clipper, a small computer . . . '

'That's the best news yet. Any watches?'

'No. They took them away. The computer was an accident. Built into a pendant the man wore around his neck. Now can you tell me what this is all about?'

'It's about getting out of here. I think we'll have enough to build what I need. Microelectronic circuitry. That's my field – or it was until they arrested me. Do the lights ever go out in here?'

'Not yet they haven't.'

'Then we'll do it the hard way. I'll want all of the stuff you have collected. I'll pass back anything I can't use. If they are taking us to Earth – how long will the trip take?'

27

'About two weeks subjective time. Half again as much in spatial time.'

'Good. I'll go slow and get it right.'

The lights were never turned off or lowered. Jan doubted if the prisoners were being watched more than casually – he had to believe that or there was no point in his even making an attempt at escape. He had sorted through the items in his pockets by touch and separated out the keys. Then, after he had lain down, he spread them out on the floor in the shelter of his body and that of the man beside him. They were small plastic tubes, in different colours, with a ring at one end. To unlock a door they were simply inserted in the hole in the face of the lock mechanism. They were so commonplace and ubiquitous, people were so used to them that they never stopped to think about the mechanism inside. Surely most people probably never even realized that there was anything contained within the apparently solid plastic.

Jan knew that there was a complex mechanism sealed inside the tubes. A microwave receiver, a microchip processor and a tiny battery. When the key was inserted in the lock a signal was transmitted by the lock circuits that activated the concealed key mechanism. A coded signal was sent by the key in return. If it was the correct one the door was unlocked, while at the same a brief but intense magnetic field recharged the battery. However if the wrong key was inserted and an incorrect code was returned not only did the lock not open, but the mechanism completely discharged the battery rendering the key useless.

Using the blade of the nail clipper, Jan shaved away carefully at the plastic. He was certain now that the job could be done. He had tools, circuitry and power supply. With patience – and skill – he should be able to build what he needed. Microchip technology was so commonplace

28

that people tended to forget that these infinitesimal microprocessors were built into every single mechanical device that they possessed. Jan was well aware of this since he had designed many circuits of this kind. He knew equally well how to alter them to his own advantage.

One of the keys was scavenged for its battery alone. The two filament-thin wires from it were used to probe the circuitry of a second key. To short out and alter the connections there. The key's transmitter became a receiver, a probe to devine the secret of the lock on the cell door. When it had been constructed to the best of his ability, Jan spoke to Debhu.

'We're ready for the first step now. I'm going to see if I can read out the lock code on this door. This would be impossible on a really sophisticated lock mechanism, so I'm hoping this one has normal interior door security.'

'You think it will work?'

Jan smiled. 'Let's say that I hope it will work. The only way I can test it is by actually trying it. But I'll need your help.'

'Anything. What do you want?'

'A little distraction for the guards. I'm not sure how closely we are being watched. But I still don't want to draw any attention to myself. I'll be at the wall near the door. I would like a couple of your men to start a fight or something at the far wall. Draw their attention for the vital seconds.'

Debhu shook his head. 'Does it have to be a fight? My people don't know anything about fighting or killing. It is not a part of our culture.'

Jan was startled. 'But all those guns you were waving around – they looked realistic enough to me.'

'Real, but unloaded. The rest was play-acting. Isn't there something else we could do? Hainault there is a gymnast. He could create a diversion.'

'Fine. Anything at all as long as it is showy.'

'I'll talk to him. When do you want him to start?'

'Now. As soon as I'm in position. I'll rub my chin, like this, when I'm ready.'

'Give me a few minutes,' Debhu said, moving slowly away across the room.

Hainault was very good and he made the most of the situation. He started with some warming up exercises, then quickly went on to handstands and backbends, all of this culminating in a gigantic backspring followed by a complete rotation in mid-air.

Before the acrobat's feet had touched down again, Jan had slipped the modified key into the hole in the lock and just as quickly withdrawn it. He strolled away from the door, the key clutched tightly in his damp fist, his shoulders hunched unconsciously as he waited for the alarm.

It did not come. After a good five minutes had gone by he knew that the first step had been successful.

The most important find, among the objects collected from the prisoners, was the microcomputer. It was a toy, a gadget, a gift undoubtedly. But for all of that it was still a computer. The guards had missed it because, to all outward appearances, it was just a piece of personal jewelry. A red stone heart on a golden chain, with a gold initial 'J' set into one side. Yet when the heart was laid on a flat surface and the 'J' depressed, a full-sized hologram of a keyboard was projected to one side. Despite the insubstantiality of the image it was still a fully operational keyboard. When a key was touched a matching magnetic field was altered and the appropriate letter or number appeared in front of the operator, also apparently floating in mid air. Despite its size it had the capacity of a normal personal computer since its memory was stored at a molecular, not a gross electronic level.

Jan now knew the code for the lock on their cell door. The next step would be to alter one of the other keys to broadcast this same code. Without the computer he could never have done this. He used it to clear the memory from the key's circuitry and then to implant the new memory. This was mostly a trial and error process, that was speeded up when he wrote a learning program for the computer that was self-correcting. It took time – but it worked, and in the end he had a key that he was sure would open the cell door without giving an alarm. Debhu looked down dubiously at the tiny cylinder of plastic.

'And you are sure that it will work?' he asked Jan.

'Fairly sure. Say ninety-nine per cent.'

'I like the odds. But after we open the inner door – then what?'

'Then we use the same key on the other door at the end of the passageway. Here the odds are greater, perhaps fifty-fifty that both locks are opened by a key with the same combination. If they are the same, why then we are through the doors and away. If not, at least we have the advantage of surprise when the outer door is opened.'

'We'll settle for that,' Debhu said. 'If this works we have you to thank for it ... '

'Don't thank me,' Jan said roughly. 'Don't do that. If we all weren't under death sentence already I would not even have considered this plan. Have you thought about what will happen if we are successful? If we get out of this cell and perhaps even manage to escape from the ship?'

'Why – we'll be free.'

Jan sighed. 'On some other world, perhaps you would be right. But this is Earth. When you get out of this spacer you'll find yourself right in the middle of a space center. Guarded, complex, sealed. Every single person you encounter will be an enemy. The proles because they will do nothing to help you – though they will surely turn you in if there is a reward being offered. All of the rest will be armed enemies. Unlike your people they know about personal combat and enjoy it. Some of them enjoy killing too. You're leaving one certain destiny for another.'

'That's our worry,' Debhu said, laying his hand on Jan's. 'We're all volunteers. We knew when we began this business of rebellion where it would probably end. Now they have us captured and mean to lead us like sheep to the slaughter. Save us from that, Jan Kulozik, and we are in your debt no matter what happens afterward.'

Jan had no words to answer with. Imprisoned, he had thought only of escape. Now, with this possibility close to hand, he was beginning to consider the consequences for the first time. They were very depressing. Yet he had to make some plan no matter how small the chance was of succeeding. He thought about this in the few days remaining before their arrival and worked out one or two possible scenarios. Lying quietly, side by side and speaking in a whisper, he explained what had to be done.

'When we leave the cell we stay close together and move very fast. Surprise is our only weapon. Once out of the cell we will have to find our way out of this ship. We may have to capture one of them, then force him to lead us . . .'

'No need. I can take care of that,' Debhu said. 'That is my work, why I commanded the food ships. I'm a construction architect. I build these things. This craft is a variation of the standard Bravos design.'

'You know your way around it?'

'In the dark.'

'Then, the important question – how do we avoid the main lock? Is there any other way out of the ship?'

'A number of them. Hatches and airlocks both, since these craft are designed to operate in and out of an atmosphere. There's a large hatch in the engine-room for heavy equipment – no, no good, takes too long to open.' He frowned in thought. 'But, yes, close by that. An access port for resupply. That's the one that we want. We can get out that way. Then what?'

Jan smiled. 'Then we see where we are and figure out what we do next. I don't even know what country we are coming down in. Probably the United States, Spaceconcent in the Mojave Desert. That presents a problem too. Let me think about it. It's a desert location with only a few road and rail connections in and out. Easy to block.'

It was after the next meal that the guards entered in force, heavily armed.

'Line up,' the officer ordered. 'Against that wall, faces to the wall. That's it, arms high, fingers spread so we can see them. First man, get your lump over here. Kneel down. Get working on him.'

They had brought a sonic razor. The prisoners were manhandled forward, one by one, and the operating head run over their faces. The ultrasonic waves gave a perfectly clean shave, severing the facial hairs without affecting the skin. It worked just as well on their heads too, removing every trace of hair from their skulls. They were shorn and humiliated; the guards thought it was very funny. The floor was thick with tufts and hanks of hair before they left. The officer called back to them.

'I want you all lying down when the warning goes. We may have up to five gees on landing and I don't want you falling around and breaking bones and giving us trouble. If you are foolish enough to get hurt you will not be repaired but will be killed. I promise you that.'

The metal door slammed behind them and the prisoners looked at each other in silence.

'Wait until after we're down and they switch from ship's gravity,' Debhu said. 'That will be when they are busiest in the shutdown routines. No one will be moving around yet and the outer hatches will still be closed.'

Jan nodded just as the alarm horn sounded.

There was vibration when the ship entered the atmosphere, then the pressure of deceleration and the rumble of distant engines sounding from the metal walls around them. A sudden tremor and they were down. They lay still, looking at Jan and Debhu.

A sudden twisting sensation pulled at them, followed by a feeling of heaviness as Earth's slightly stronger gravitational field took hold.

'Now!' Debhu said.

Jan had been lying next to the door. He was on his feet instantly and pushing the key into the lock; the door swung open easily in his hand. The short hall beyond was empty. He sprinted the length of it, aware of the others close behind him, slammed his weight against the door at the end – then carefully slid the key into the opening in the lock. Holding his breath.

The door unlocked. No alarms were sounded that they were aware of. He nodded to Debhu who grabbed the door and hurled it open.

'This way!' he called out, sprinting down the empty corridor. A spaceman walked around the bend, saw them and tried to run. He was overwhelmed, crushed down, held, then pounded into unconsciousness by Jan's bare fists.

'We're armed now,' Debhu said, tearing the pistol from the man's holster. 'Take it, Jan. You know more about it's use than we do.'

Debhu was up on the instant and they were close behind him. He ignored the lift shaft, too slow, and instead hurled himself down the emergency stairwell, risking a fall with every leap. When he reached the door at the bottom he stopped and let the others catch up.

'This opens into the main engine compartment,' he said. 'There will be at least four ratings and an officer there. Do we try to take them, knock them down ...'

'No.' Jan said. 'Too risky. They may be armed and they could sound the alarm. Where would the officer be?'

'At the ancillary control panel. To your left about four metres away.'

'Fine. I'll go first. Fan out behind me but don't get between me and any of the crew if you can prevent it.'

'You mean ...' Debhu said.

'You know exactly what I mean,' Jan said, raising the gun. 'Open the door.'

The officer was very young and his frightened cry, then scream of pain before the second shot silenced him, brought the escaping prisoners to a stumbling halt. Only Jan ran on. The engines were lightly manned. He had to murder only two other men; the second by shooting him in the back.

'Come on!' Jan shouted. 'It's clear.'

They kept their faces averted from his as they ran by, following Debhu to the hatch. He did not waste time looking for the electrical controls but instead seized the manual emergency wheel and began turning. After two turns he was pushed aside by Hainault who used his athelete's muscles to whirl the wheel, over and over, until the latches clicked free.

'And no alarm yet,' Jan said. 'Push it open and see if there is any kind of welcome waiting for us outside.'

# Chapter Five

It was dark and quiet in the landing pit, the only sounds were the click of contracting metal and the drip of water. The air was warm but not hot, the hull and pit itself had been cooled by the water sprays after landing. Jan led the way, through the open hatch and onto the wide metal gangway that had extended automatically after the landing. They were at least fifty metres above the pit bottom that was still boiling with steam. High above them there were harsh lights and the sound of machinery, engines.

'There should be exit doors near the water jets,' Debhu whispered. 'If these pits are designed like the ones I'm familiar with.'

'Let's hope they are,' Jan said. 'You had better show us the way.'

He stood aside as Debhu led the others past, looking on all sides for any sign of pursuit. Their escape must have been discovered by this time.

The lights flared on, set into the rim of the pit above, bright as the unshielded sun of Halvmörk. An instant later the guns began firing. Rocket powered slugs ricochetted and screamed off the concrete and steel, sent up explosions of water from the puddles. Tore through the soft flesh of human bodies.

Jan shielded his eyes with his arm as he fired upwards, blindly. Throwing the gun aside and falling backwards when his ammunition was exhausted. By a miracle of chance he was unharmed as yet – hoarse screams brutally informed him that the others weren't that lucky. His shoulder crashed painfully into a metal support and he sought shelter behind it, trying to blink away the floating spots of light before his eyes.

He was only three metres from the hatch they had used to flee from the ship into this bullet-filled trap. Their escape had not gone unnoticed; the guards had taken instant revenge. There was only death in this pit. Trying to ignore the rain of bullets, Jan ran forward and fell through the open hatch.

It was an act of instinct, to escape the sure death outside. He lay on the hard steel for a moment, knowing that he had not escaped but just postponed his destruction. But they could not find him like this, not just lying here waiting to be captured or shot. He scrambled to his feet and stumbled back into the engine room. It was populated only by the dead. But the lift door across the room was opening . . .

Jan dived for the bank of instruments against the bulkhead, jammed himself into the narrow space behind them, pushing back deeper and deeper as the many thudding footsteps came close.

'Hold it right there,' a voice ordered. 'You'll get blown away by our own men.'

The murmur of voices was cut short by the same man again. 'Quiet in the ranks.' Then more softly. 'Lauca here, come in command. Do you read me command . . . Yes, sir. Ready in the engine room. Yes, firing stopping now. Right, we'll mop up. No survivors.' Then he shouted aloud as the gunfire ceased in the pit outside.

'Try not to shoot each other in your enthusiasm – but I want those rebels wasted. Understand. No survivors. And leave them where they fall for the media cameras. The Major wants the world to see what happens to rebels and murderers. Go!'

They streamed by shouting angrily, guns ready. Jan could do nothing except wait for one of them to glance aside, to see for just one instant what was behind the instrument board. No one did. Their guns were ready for the vengeance awaiting them outside. The officer came last.

He stopped not an arm's distance from Jan, but staring intently after the troops, then spoke into the microphone on his collar.

'Hold all firing from the rim, repeat hold firing. Mop up troops are now in the pit.'

Jan sidled forward – and his shirt caught on a protruding bolthead, held an instant, then ripped free. The officer heard the slight sound and turned his head. Jan lunged forward and seized him by the throat with both hands.

It was unscientific and crude. But it worked. The officer thrashed about, trying to kick Jan, to tear his fingers from his throat. They fell and the man's helmet went rolling away. He tore at the throttling hands, his fingernails tearing bleeding welts in Jan's skin, his mouth gasping for air that he could not breathe. But Jan's muscles were strengthened by hard work, his fingers squeezing even tighter now with the desperate fear of failure. One of them would live; one die. His thumbs bit deep into the flesh of the officer's neck and he looked with no compassion into the wide and bulging eyes.

He held on until he was sure that the man was dead, until there was no trace of a pulse under his thumb.

Reason returned – and with it fear. He looked around wildly. There was no one else there. Outside the firing was becoming more spasmodic as the soldiers ran out of targets. They would be back, someone else might enter soon . . . He tore at the officer's clothing, ripping open the magnetic fasteners, pulling the boots from his feet. It took less than a minute to strip the man, to throw off his own clothes and pull on the uniform. The fit was adequate though the boots were tight. The hell with that. He jammed the helmet on his head then stuffed the limp corpse and discarded clothing behind the instrument bank where he had hidden, pushing it as far back as he could. Time, time, there was not enough of it. As he ran towards the lift he fumbled with the chin strap of the helmet. His thumb was raised to the button when he looked at the indicator.

It was on the way down.

The emergency stairs, the way they had entered. He slammed through the door and pushed hard against the mechanism to make it close faster. Now. Up the stairs. Not too quickly, don't want to be out of breath. How far? What deck? Where would there be an exit from the ship? Debhu would know. But Debhu was dead. They were all dead. He tried to blame himself for their deaths as he stumbled on the treads, but he could not. Murdered here or murdered later. It was all the same. But he was still free and it would not be as simple to kill him as it had been to slaughter the unarmed men in the pit – who did not even know how to fight. Jan loosened the officer's pistol in the holster. Well he knew how. It would not be that easy with him.

How many decks had he climbed? Four, five. One was as good as any other. He laid his hand on the next door and took a deep breath, then pulled his uniform down. Shoulders back, another breath – then through the door.

The corridor was empty. He walked down it at what he hoped was a brisk military pace. There was a junction ahead and one of the crewmen came around it. He nodded at Jan and started to hurry by. Jan put out his hand and stopped him.

'Just a minute my good man.' The accents of his prep school, long forgotten, sprang instantly to his lips. 'Where is the nearest exit?'

The crewman started to pull away, eyes widening. Jan spoke again, more firmly.

'Speak up. I came into this ship from the pit. Now how do I get out to report?'

'Oh, sorry your honour. I didn't know. Up one deck, that's the stairwell over there. Then right and first right again.'

Jan nodded and walked stiffly away. So far so good. He had fooled the spaceman – but would this bluff work with any others he met? He would find out soon enough. What had the dead officer called himself? He dredged his memory. Loka? No, Lauca, or something very close to that. He glanced at the ring on the uniform cuff. Sub-Lieutenant Lauca. Jan pushed open the door and climbed the flight of steps.

It was only when he had turned the corner that he saw the two guards stationed at the exit from the ship. The airlock controls had been overriden and both interior and exterior locks were open. Beyond the outer lock a metal bridge led across the pit to safety.

The guards snapped to attention, slamming their heels down and bringing their weapons to port arms. He could only go forward towards them now, even when they stepped in front of him. Jan walked steadily on to stop before them. And noticed something of utmost importance.

Their unit numbers were different from the ones on the uniform he wore.

'I am Lieutenant Lauca. Mop-up squad. My radio is dead. Where is your commanding officer?'

They snapped to attention as he spoke.

'The major is down there, sir. Command post in the company office.'

'Thank you.'

Jan returned the salute in the correct manner that had

been drilled into him with great precision during his cadet days at school, wheeled smartly about and stamped away.

As soon as he was out of sight of the airlock he turned in the opposite direction, away from the command post, and walked off between the machines and harsh lights and on into the night.

Not that he was free. He knew better than to believe that for an instant. No one was really free on Earth with its ubiquitous webs of surveillance spreading completely about the globe. The lieutenant's body would be found soon, that was certain. The man's uniform would be an asset until that moment – but after it a terrible liability. And he didn't even know where on Earth he was. Probably Spaceconcent at Mojave, though he could not be sure. The military might very well have their own bases kept secret from the public. But that wasn't important, not now. The first order of business was getting off the base. There was a road of some kind off to his left, well lit with occasional vehicles going by, and he went in that direction.

From the shelter of some large crates he looked out at the brightly lit gate. It would need more than bluff to get through this one. Perhaps he ought to try the fence, although he knew that there was no way through this without setting off a number of alarms. Speed. Whatever he did he had to do it fast.

*'Lieutenant Lauca, come in'*

He started as the voice sounded loudly inside his head. Transmitted by the bone conduction field inside the helmet. The radio, of course. Now where would the switch be? He fumbled at his belt, finding the radio controls, trying to make them out in the dark.

*'Lauca, come in.'*

Was this the right one? It seemed to be. Only one way to find out .. he pressed it and spoke.

'Yes, sir.'

*'That's enough. We want some remains for the press. Call your men back.'*

The commander's voice died away and the carrier tone vanished. The ruse worked, he had gained a few minutes – but no more. He switched the radio to broadchannel reception and listened with one ear to the commands passing back and forth. He must do something, even something desperate. And fast.

Jan ran forward to the illuminated traffic lane and waited out of sight of the guards at the exit. A car came towards him, there was someone next to the driver though and Jan faded back out of sight. A motorcycle was close behind the car. The nothing more. Seconds, then minutes ticked away. There seemed to be a steady stream of traffic into the base but nothing at all going out. The radio murmured in his ear. Routine commands. No emergencies yet. Something, anything!

There! A flatbed truck with a heavy load lashed in the back. He couldn't see inside the high cab. It was a chance he had to take.

Jan stepped out in front of the slowly moving truck and raised his hand. Standing, unmoving, as it braked to a stop. The driver leaned out of his window.

'Can I help your honour?'

'Yes. Has this vehicle been searched yet?'

'No, sir.'

'Then open the other door. I'm coming up.'

Jan climbed the ladder and swung in through the open door. The driver, beefy and middle aged, roughly dressed and wearing a cloth cap, was all alone. Jan slammed the door shut, turned back to the man and drew the pistol.

'Do you know what this is?'

'Yes your honour, I know, yes I do.'

The man was stammering with fear, staring wide-eyed at the muzzle of the pistol. Jan could not afford to feel sorry for him.

'Good. Then do exactly as I say. Drive through the gate as you always do. Say nothing. I shall be on the floor and will kill you if you so much as open your mouth. Do you believe that?'

'Yes, I do! I certainly do ...'

'Start driving.'

The turbine whined under the hood as they started forward. They moved for awhile, they must be close, then the driver touched the brakes. Jan pushed the gun up between the driver's legs and hoped that the raw fear in the man's face could not be seen by the guards below. A voice said something indistinct and the driver took a sheaf of papers from the door pocket and passed them down. And waited. Jan could see the sweat streaming down his face to drip from his double chin. He did not move the gun.

The papers were handed back and the driver let them drop from his fingers to the floor as he kicked the truck into gear and rolled it forward. They drove for less than a minute before a loud voice sounded in Jan's ears, overriding the murmurs of all the others.

*'Emergency. An officer has been killed, a sub-lieutenant. His uniform is missing. All patrols, all units, check in with your commanders. All gates sealed at once.'*

They were just that little bit too late.

# Chapter Six

The truck was out of sight of the gate, but still on the main road, passing now through a dark and deserted warehouse area illuminated only by wide-spaced street lights.

'Turn at the next corner,' Jan ordered. There was a good chance that pursuit might be close behind them. 'And again at the next corner. Stop.'

The air brakes hissed and the truck shuddered to a halt. They were in a back street, a hundred metres from the nearest light. Perfect.

'What time is it?' Jan asked.

The driver hesitated, then glanced at his watch. 'Three . . . in the morning . . . ' He stammered.

'I'm not going to hurt you. Don't worry.' He tried to reassure the frightened man; he also did not lower his gun. 'What time is dawn?'

'About six.'

Three hours of darkness then. Not very much time. But it was all he had. Another, even more important question. 'Where are we?'

'Dinkstown. All warehouses. No one lives here.'

'Not that. The base back there. What's its name?'

The driver gaped at Jan as though he had lost his mind, but finally answered. 'Mojave, your honour. The space center. In the Mojave desert . . '

'That's enough.' Jan had decided on the next step. It was dangerous, but he needed transportation. And everything was dangerous now. 'Take your clothes off.'

'Please, no, I don't want to be killed . . !'

'Stop it! I said you wouldn't be hurt. What's your name?'

'Millard, your honour. Eddie Millard.'

'Here's what I'm going to do, Eddie. I'm going to take your clothes and this truck and tie you up. I'm not going to injure you. When they find you, or you get lose, just tell them everything that happened. You won't get in any trouble ... '

'No? I'm in that trouble now.' There was despair as well as anger in the man's voice. 'Might as well be dead. I'm out of a job, the least of it. On the welfare. Police will talk to me. Might be better off dead!'

He shouted the last words hysterically and reached over to clutch at Jan in the seat next to him. He was very strong. Jan had no recourse. The gun caught the driver in the forehead, then a second time when he still kept struggling. Eddie Millard sighed deeply and slumped, unconscious. What he had said was true, Jan realized as he struggled to strip off the man's clothes. One more victim. Are we all victims? There wasn't enough time now to think about things like that.

As he pushed the heavy man from the cab, lowering him as best he could to the roadway, Jan began to shake. Too much had happened, too quickly. He had murdered too many men. It was a brutal galaxy and he was turning into another one of the brutes. No! He wouldn't accept that. The means never justified the ends – but he had been fighting solely in self-defence. From the time he had sacrificed his comfortable position here on Earth, there had been no turning back. When he had discovered that he had been one of the captors in a police state he had made a decision. Personally, he had lost a lot. But there were others who believed as he did – and the galaxy-wide rebellion had been the result. It was war now, and he was a soldier. For the moment it had to be just that simple.

Recriminations would come after victory. And the revolutionaries would triumph, had to triumph. He dare consider no other outcome.

Eddie Millard's clothes stank of old sweat, were big as a tent wrapped about him. They would just have to do. The cap would conceal his new-shaven head. And there was no thought of possibly jamming the man into the stolen uniform. His stained underwear would have to suffice. There was some insulated wire behind the seat and he used this to secure the unconscious man's hands. That would do well enough. he would have to abandon the truck very soon in any case. Run, that's all he could do, just run.

The engine ground to life when he turned the key and the truck moved slowly down the narrow street. Jan was wearing the stolen officer's helmet, there was no other way of hearing the military radio, but after a few minutes he realized that it was a waste of time. There were a few distant signals, and even these died away. The military knew that he had the stolen radio so the communication computer was changing all of the frequencies to cut him off from their radioed commands. He threw the helmet to the floor and stepped on the accelerator, slowing down only when he saw an intersection ahead with a main road. Computerized traffic control changed the light to green as he approached, letting him merge with the sporadic traffic. Most of it large rigs like his. There were signs for a freeway ahead, 395 to Los Angeles, but he went right by the entrance. He would have no chance at all of getting through the police check at the outskirts of the built up area.

There were brighter lights coming up now, and a heavy semi approaching from the opposite direction cut in front of him so that he had to slow down. Good. A fuel area with parking behind it, an all-night restuarant of some kind. He

46

turned in, going slowly, past the group of vehicles and on towards a darkened building beyond. It was a garage. Locked now, and he could just get his rig behind it. It would do. At least it would be safe there for awhile; with a little luck it might be some hours before it was found. What next?

Keep moving. He had Eddie Millard's identification, but that would be good only for the most casual inspection. And a purse with some money in it. Bank notes, a handful of change. He stuffed them into his pocket, pulling at the clothes so they didn't look obviously ill-fitting. If the proles here were anything like those back in Britain he doubted if this outfit would even be noticed. Fine. But what about the officer's uniform? Worthless. The alarm would be out for that. But the gun and extra clips of bullets? No, he couldn't part with them. He rooted under the seat and behind it until he found a grimy sack. It would have to do. He stuffed the gun and ammunition into it, then pushed the discarded uniform and helmet out of sight behind the seat. With the gun under his arm he got out, locked the cab, then climbed down. Then threw the keys over the fence. There was little else he could do. Drawing a deep breath he started forward, walking slowly through the warm night air towards the lights of the restaurant.

Jan stood in the concealing darkness, hesitating, unsure of the next step. He was tired and thirsty – no, not tired, completely exhausted now that he thought about it. From the time when he had opened the cell door he had been on the run, in deadly danger most of the time. Adrenalin had kept him going, had masked the growing fatigue. He felt it now, staggering at the release of tension, lurching forward to lean against the wall of the restaurant. His eyes were on a level with the bottom of the window and he could look in. A large room, booths and tables, a counter with two men sitting at it; otherwise empty. Should he take a chance and go in? It was a risk, but everything was a risk. Some food, something to eat, a chance to sit for a few moments and get his thoughts together. He needed it. Fatigue was making him fatalistic. He would be caught in the end – but at least when he was taken he would have a full stomach. Pushing away from the wall he walked to the entrance steps, up them and into the building.

During his other visits to the United States – how many years ago? – he had seen nothing like this place. Of course he had been at the best restaurants in New York City and Detroit, so he had nothing to judge by. The floor was concrete, stained and ancient. The men at the counter did not bother to look up or glance at him when he slipped into the booth nearest the door. The table and seat seemed to be made of aluminium, dented and worn with time. How did one order, by going to the counter? Or was there a selector and delivery mechanism at the table? It had a transparent top, now almost translucent with scratches, with a menu beneath it. Under DRINKS coffee was listed, but no tea. A number of strange items followed the EATS heading. The meaning of the word was obvious, but it seemed an unusual construction. He tried touching the coffee entry but this did not seem to do anything. Looking around he noticed the button on the wall under a TV screen. It read RING FOR SERVICE. He put out a tentative finger and pressed it.

In the silence of the room a buzzer could be heard sounding somewhere behind the counter. Neither of the diners moved. But a moment later a girl came around the counter and walked towards him. She had a slate in one hand. Personal service in a place like this! Her uniform was faded and as stained as the floor, nor was she as young as she had looked at a distance. Her coarse hair was touched with grey and she apparently was toothless; no recommendation for the quality of the food.

'What'll it be?' she asked, looking at Jan with complete disinterest.

'Coffee.'

'Anything to eat?'

He looked back at the menu and stabbed a finger down.

'Hamburger.'

'With the works?'

He nodded, having not the slightest idea what she meant, which appeared to satisfy her because she scrawled on the slate then went away. He had never had a hamburger in his life, had not even the slightest idea what it was. But he knew that his accent was English, and decidedly public school English at that. So when he read the menu that word had leaped out at him. Hamburger. An old joke when he was a boy, with his mates, a line from a long lost American film. 'Gimme a hamboygah.' They said it a lot. Apparently this bit of regional accent still made sense.

One of the men at the counter put some coins down on it, their clinking drawing Jan's attention. He stood and started for the door, glancing at Jan as he went by. Had his eyes widened sightly at the same time? There was no way of telling because he pushed on out into the night. Could he have recognized Jan? How? Or was Jan just being paranoid? He moved the sack closer to him on the seat and shook the mouth open so he could reach the gun easily. Instead of worrying about every stranger he knew that he should be thinking about ways of escape.

When the food arrived some minutes later he had not even the glimmer of a plan. After the waitress had served him she looked pointedly at his clothes.

'That'll be six bucks even.'

Cash on the line, dressed as he was. Jan didn't blame her. He dug out the handful of green notes and put them on the table, extracting a five and a one and passing them over to her. She shoved them into the pocket of her apron and left.

The coffee was hot and delicious, burning a wakeful track down his throat. The hamburger a different matter entirely. It appeared to be a bap of some kind with stuffing. There was no knife or fork and Jan had not the slightest idea of how to go about eating it. In the end, sure that no one was watching him, he seized it up and took a bite. It was very different from anything that he had ever tasted before, but interesting nevertheless. Buried in its heart was a layer of barely cooked mince which had a number of sauces and bits of salad spread over it. But it was immensely satisfying too. He wolfed it down. It took him only a few minutes to eat it and he was finishing the coffee when the two men came in.

Without looking around and without hesitation they slid into the booth across the table from him. Jan put the coffee cup slowly down and seized the butt of the pistol with his other hand.

They weren't looking at him; appeared not to notice him. One of them took a coin from his pocket and reached over to put it into a slot under the table TV screen. The machine came to life with a blare of music. Jan did not look at it; he drew the gun from the bag under the shelter of the table. The thin man who had inserted the coin touched the controls, changing channels until he was satisfied, then sat back. It was a sports broadcast, about a racing match of some kind.

What did it mean? Jan thought. Both men were middle aged, dressed very much the way he was. They appeared to be examining the menu, but did not press the service button. As yet neither of them had caught his eye. The words of the television announcer cut suddenly through his concentration.

' . . . further news of the criminal rebels who attempted to seize the *Alpharon*. The fighting has ended and the murderers have met the fate they wished for others. Quick justice at the hands of the comrades of those brave men who gave their lives for their home world . . . '

One glimpse of the torn, twisted and blood-drenched bodies of his friends was enough. Jan looked back at the two men. The announcer's next words froze him motionless.

'One criminal escaped. His name is Jan Kulozik and the public is warned that he is dangerous. He is wanted alive for questioning concerning details of this mutinous plot. There is a reward of twenty-five thousand dollars for anyone supplying information that might lead to his recapture. All citizens of California and Arizona are warned to be on the lookout for this man . . . '

Jan permitted himself one swift look at the screen. There was his face, full front and profile. Taken years ago before he was shipped from Earth, but instantly recognizable. When he looked back he found that the two men were now looking straight at him.

They both had their hands on the table so they were either very sure of themselves – or very stupid.

'Is all that true, what he said?' The thin man spoke for the first time. Jan did not answer so after awhile he added. 'Why do they want you, Kulozik?'

Jan's answer was to bring the barrel of the gun up over the edge of the table.

'This is a standard issue 65 calibre, rifleless pistol. It fires rocket slugs that can blow a hole through a cow. I want you to stand up and walk out of here ahead me. Now.'

They obeyed instantly, sliding out of the booth and

waiting for him, their backs turned. Then they went out the door with Jan following them. As he walked through after them Jan was barely aware of the figure in the darkness to one side, swinging something. He half turned and was just bringing up the gun, when he was struck.

# Chapter Seven

'I can only repeat what I've told you before,' Jan said.

'Then do it.'

It was a different voice – but the questions were the same. Jan was bound so tightly to the hard chair that his arms and legs were numb; his eyes were bandaged. It seemed that he had been tied there for eternity.

'My name is Jan Kulozik. I arrived on the *Alpharon*. I didn't know the ship's name until I heard the broadcast. I was with a group of prisoners who escaped. I was the only one that got away. I killed an officer . . . '

'His name?'

'Lauca, Sub-Lieutenant Lauca. And it was not murder but self-defence. I've told you all this already. I took his uniform and gun, comandeered a truck driven by a man named Eddie Millard. I left the truck behind the garage before going into the restaurant where you jumped me. Now you tell me something. Who are you? You're Security, aren't you?'

'Shut up. We ask the questions . . . '

The man's voice broke off as someone else entered the room. There were footsteps and muttered voices. They came towards him – and his face burned with pain as the adhesive tape that covered his eyes was torn away. He gasped with shock and kept his eyes shut against the searing light.

'What was the registration number of the last car you owned in England?'

'How the hell do I know? That was a long time ago.' He blinked at the three men standing before him. Two of them were the ones from the restaurant. 'If you're Security then you know all about me. So why these games?'

The newcomer, a scrawny man with a head as naturally bald as Jan's shaved one, answered him. 'We're not Security. But maybe you are. A plant. To find our people. So you should answer our questions. We can help you – if you are what you say you are. If not, we'll kill you.'

Jan looked at their faces, then nodded slowly.

'I feel the same hesitancy on my own part. You could be Security no matter what you say. So I will tell you only what is in my record. I'll not compromise others.'

'Agreed.' The bald man looked at a sheaf of printout. 'What was your phone number in London?'

Jan closed his eyes, tried to think. It was another age, really another life. He visualized his apartment, the doorman, the lift. Going into his flat, picking up the phone . . .

'Oh one . . two three six . . treble one two. That's it.'

There were more questions like this. He answered them more quickly as memory flooded back. That must be his security file they held – but how had they obtained it? Only Security would have that. Were they just playing with him?

'That's enough,' the bald man said, throwing aside the accordion folded paper. 'Cut him loose. We'll just have to take a chance that he's telling the truth.'

They had to hold Jan up when the ropes were removed. Until feeling – and pain – returned to his numbed body. He rubbed at his sore legs. 'Fine,' he said. 'You're satisfied. But as far as I know you are still Security.'

'For our job, we don't carry IDs,' baldy said, smiling for the first time. 'So you will just have to act as though we are. If you are a Security plant let me tell you, truthfully, that we know no others in the underground. That's why we were picked for this job. There must be one of the brotherhood in the police – that's where this printout came from. My party name is Shiny.' He pointed to his hairless skull and smiled again. This time Jan smiled in return.

'I hope that you're telling the truth, Shiny. If you are Security you can find out everything that I know without all this rigmarole. I know. I've been through it.'

'And you've been to the other worlds?' one of the men blurted out, unable to contain himself further. 'The rebellion. Tell us about it. All we know is the official propaganda.'

'What do they say?'

'Nothing. Hogwash. Misled few ... rebellion put down. Saboteurs have destroyed food crops so there will be rationing. All of the rebels captured or destroyed ... '

'Hogwash – just like you said. They wouldn't dare tell you that we've won! They have been kicked off every world and have fled back here to Earth.'

Their stern faces changed while he talked, relaxing, smiling – then shouting with glee.

'You mean it – you actually mean it?'

'I've no cause to lie. They rule here in the solar system – but nowhere else.'

It was Christmas, holiday time, all of the pleasures of the world rolled into one. If they are faking this, Jan thought, they are the best actors in the world. He was sure now that he had fallen into the hands of the resistance instead of the police. He told them all that he knew, then finally interrupted the flow of questions.

'It's my turn,' he said. 'How was it that you got to me ahead of Security?'

'Just luck,' Shiny told him. 'Or maybe there are more of us. As soon as they began broadcasting that flash about you the word came down to try and find you. We have more sympathizers than members. One of them saw you here and got through to us. The rest you know.'

'So – what comes next?'

'You can be very important to the cause, Jan. If you agree to work with us.'

There was a wry twist in Jan's answering smile. 'That's how I got into this trouble in the first place. I don't see why not. My future will be short with a very unhappy ending if I don't have help from someone.'

'Good. Then we're getting you out of here at once. Before they discover that you're being helped. I don't know how it's being done – nor do I want to. We have some clothes here for you. Put them on while I make a call.'

Jan pulled on the sleezy cotton slacks and shirt. He was glad to be rid of the military boots which were hurting even more now. The open sandals were a relief. One of the men went out and brought back a peaked cap that had *Dodgers* printed on it in yellow script letters.

'Take this,' he said. 'Cover that shaven head until your hair grows back in. Got some rotgut bourbon here. Be mighty pleased if you would drink with us.'

'My pleasure,' Jan said, taking a plastic beaker of the pale fluid. It was very strong. 'Here's to freedom. May Earth some day share it with the stars.'

'That's something to drink to.'

Jan was on his third glass of bourbon – it tasted better and he felt better with each glass – by the time Shiny came back.

'Gotta move fast,' he said. 'Someone's waiting for you. We'll have to walk. Everything on wheels is being searched.'

It wasn't far, and the night air cleared Jan's head. Through dark back streets all the way. Shiny kept looking at his watch and made them run the last few blocks.

56

'Got to be there at a certain time. I'll leave you in front of a door. As soon as I'm out of sight, you knock on it. You'll be let in. Good luck, Jan. This is the place.'

It appeared to be a small side entrance in a very large building. He shook hands quickly and moved away. Jan knocked once, lightly, and the door opened. It was dark inside.

'Come on, quick,' a voice whispered. The darkness was even deeper when the door closed behind him.

'Listen carefully,' the unseen man said. 'You go through that door and you're in a garage. Full of trailers. They're all going out tonight. Everyone of them is sealed because they've been in bond. They won't be searched. The third one from the door, the back is opened. Go there and get in. We got seals so they'll never know its been opened. Get in, I'll come and close it. It's important you shouldn't see my face. Someone will get you out the other end, in LA. Look natural now when you go out there. Maybe others around, but no one will bother you if you look natural. And don't let them see you getting into the thing or you have had it. Stand there while I take a look.'

Another door opened a crack and Jan could see the outline of a man's head against the light. He looked for a short time, then moved aside.

'Quick now,' the voice said. 'And good luck.'

The building was gigantic, echoing with the distant hammer of a loud exhaust. Rows of trailers, each with a large shipping container secured to it, stretched into the distance. He walked towards the nearest one, slowly as though he belonged there. The sound of the exhaust died away to be replaced by the clang of metal upon metal. He looked around casually when he reached the third trailer; there was no one in sight. He pulled open the heavy door and climbed in. As he pulled the door shut behind him he had a quick glimpse of stacked boxes filling most of the body of the trailer, leaving an area just big enough for him. A few minutes later the door was slammed all the way shut from the outside and locked into place.

It was dark, warm and slightly musty. He sat down with his back against the wall, but found that this was hard and uncomfortable. Lying down was better and he pillowed his head on his arm. He was asleep without knowing it, nor did he stir when a tractor backed into place and sealed itself to the trailer. The big rig lurched into easy motion and out onto the road; Jan slept on. Waking only when they shuddered to a stop, air brakes hissing. Jan was pulled awake, blinking into the darkness, feeling a cold stab of fear until he remembered what had happened, where he was. He caught his breath as someone outside rattled the bars that sealed the door. When they opened it he would be caught and that would be the end of everything. He crouched there in the darkness, waiting – and relaxed only when the rig lurched into motion again. If that had been the checkpoint, then they were safely through. Tension drained away as they kept rolling, not stopping again. The motion lulled him to sleep and he welcomed it gladly, did not fight against it.

Jan stirred on the hard surface but did not waken completely until the next time the truck stopped. There was a short wait, then they started up again. A police check before entering a city? This was what would have been done in Britain; there was a good chance the same security procedures might be used here. The next time they stopped Jan could hear rattling again at the door seals next to him and he was ready when the door swung open. He shielded his eyes with his hand under the onslaught of tropical light.

'Come on out, Buster, this is the end of the line for you,' a hoarse voice said. Jan slid to the ground and squinted through the glare at the uniformed policeman who stood in front of him. Captured! He turned, started to run, and the man's large hand seized him by the arm and swung him about.

'No games! Just get into the back of the black and white and lie on the floor. They made me break my cover for you, Buster, and it had better be worth it.' He pulled Jan forward as he talked, then shoved him in the direction of a black and white car that was heavily festooned with lights and sirens, parked behind the tractor trailer in the narrow alleyway. The rear door was open and Jan got in and dropped to the floor as the door was slammed behind him. A moment later the policeman climbed into the front and they reversed out of the alley at high speed, braked to a squealing stop, then shot off down the road. Once they were moving the driver relaxed and looked over his shoulder at Jan.

'Is it true, what you told them, that all of the planets are, like, what do you call it . . ?'

'Free. Yes, they are. It was a rebellion that could not be stopped.'

'Well that's good to hear. Maybe it's catching and we'll get a bit of it here on old mother Earth. They could sure use some of it where you're going. I'm turning you over to the spooks. I don't know how comfortable you're going to be there, but you'll be safe enough for a while.'

Spooks? Jan thought. Ghosts? What was the man talking about. 'I'm afraid that I'm not acquainted with the term.'

'You sound like a Limey. Are you? A Brit?'

'Yes, I was born in England. I left there some time ago.'

'You sounded like one, you know, the way they talk in the flicks. Well I don't know how things work over where you come from, Mr Limey, but over here, well, things I

59

guess are different. We're going to New Watts. When you see it you'll know what I'm talking about. Take a look. I'll stop and you just lift your nose up and see for yourself.'

They drove on, slowly, then eased to a stop. 'All right, now,' the policeman said.

Jan rose up carefully to see that they had parked beside a row of small homes. They had been attractive once, but now they were collapsed and tumbledown, windows knocked out and roofs sagging. On the other side of the street was a high wire fence with a wasteland behind it, mounds of burned earth with only the occasional bit of grass or weed growing there. A good hundred metres beyond was another, identical fence. On the other side of this were buildings; homes and office blocks. Jan couldn't see any details clearly but they definitely had a ramshackle look.

'Get back down,' the policeman ordered. 'That's where you're going. Don't look so bad from here ... ' He laughed, not humourously but more like an ironic comment. 'Going through a checkpoint now. But all the guys there know me and they'll just wave. I'll give him a blast so they'll think that it's a call.'

The car surged forward and the siren began to wail. They turned, picked up speed, and bumped over something hard in the road, then went on. After a bit the siren was killed and their headlong pace slowed.

'Get ready,' the policeman said. 'I'm going to go along real easy, but not stop all the way. You bail out when I tell you to. You'll be next to a kind of little back alley between some yards. Walk down it nice and slow and you'll be met.'

'Thanks for the help.'

'Don't thank me until you see what you got into. Now!'

Jan pulled the handle and pushed the door open. He

stepped out and it was torn from his hand as the car accelerated, the sudden motion slamming the door shut. The police car spun around the next corner and vanished from sight. Jan looked at the wooden, rickety fences stretched away on both sides of a packed dirt lane. He followed instructions and walked down it, feeling that he was being watched, but seeing no one. There were doors let into the fencing and as he passed one it swung open.

'Get in here,' a rough voice said.

Jan turned to look at the man, at the two others with him. All three carried pistols, pointing at him. All three of them had coal-black skins.

# Chapter Eight

'Are you the one they say come in the starship?' The nearest man asked. Jan nodded and the man waved the gun. 'Then come on in so's you can tell us all about it.'

They crowded around him, pushing him into the house and down a dank corridor to an interior room. Behind him he heard bolts rattling shut. The room had sealed windows and was airless, unfurnished except for a round wooden table surrounded by ramshackle chairs. One of the men pulled him by the arm, dragging him to a chair, then waved his long and well worn pistol in Jan's face.

'You a spy,' he said angrily, grating the words through his clamped teeth. 'You ofay spy . . . '

'Come away now, nuf of dat,' an older man said, pulling gently at the angry man's shoulder. He moved away reluctantly and the older man sat down across from Jan.

'Trouble is the bolly dogs brung you here, he don't like it. Who does? I'm Willy. You called Jan, saw your picture on television.'

Jan nodded, straining to understand the other man's words. He was speaking in dialect, as thick and incomprehensible to him as Glaswegian.

'The teevee say you from the stars. If that true, you tell us what happening out there.'

Once again Jan told about the success of the rebellion, and while he spoke the man leaned forward, listening intensely, making him repeat things; apparently his accent was equally difficult for them to understand. Fatigue began to catch up with him again and his throat grew dry.

When he asked for some water, Willy signalled to one of the men.

'You hungry too?' he asked. Jan nodded and Willy called instructions through the open door.

The food was unfamiliar but filling. Boiled greens of some kind, white beans with black spots on them, and a slab of some sort of highly seasoned meat substitute. The men watched him while he ate and talked excitedly among themselves.

'What they wants to know,' Willy asked. 'Is they any brothers in the star people.'

'I don't understand.'

'Black. Black people like us. Or is this more whitey fightin' an' killin' each one the other.'

This was the important question and the room was silent as Jan finished his meal and pushed the dish away.

'Thank you. I was very hungry.' He thought for a moment. 'First, just one question myself. Is everyone here in, what's the name? New Watts? Are they all black.'

'You better believe it!'

'That's not the way on the planets. I mean I have never before seen people separated by their skin colour. Here on Earth, yes, there are different skin colours among the indigenous populations of Africa and Asia, that is, there are divisions by racial types on a purely geographical basis. But once people have been transported to the planets these separations break down. They don't matter. There are enough other things to worry about . . .'

'You talkin' a little fast,' Willy said. 'Do I catch you saying they all colour blind out there? All kind of skins mix together?'

'Yes. Of course. Skin colour doesn't matter you see.'

'Sure matter here!' Willy said and slapped his knee and

all of the men laughed aloud at this. Jan smiled, not quite sure what the joke was.

'Just hope you is tellin' the truth,' Willy said, and one of the men shouted 'Amen!' very loud. 'Jes hard to believe, that's all. I think you better talk to the Preacher. He kinda talk your language. He'll tell us what is what.'

Jan was led from the room by the man, still carrying their guns. The weapons were all old and worn, museum pieces. They entered another room in the house, a bedroom where small black children sat on the patched quilts of a bed. They and an old and white-haired woman followed their passage in staring silence. There was an exit here, a rough-edge hole that had been chopped through the wall. It led into a covered passage to another house. When they had passed through four separate dwellings in this manner Jan realized that the houses must all be connected like this, making one extended building. They finally came to a closed door on which Willy knocked lightly.

'Come in,' a voice called out. Jan was hustled through the door into an extensive, book-lined room. The difference from the other quarters he had seen was striking. This could well have been his old tutor's study at university, resembling it in more ways than one. The desk was thick with papers and opened books, there were framed drawings on the walls, and even a globe of the world. Soft chairs and there, behind the desk, the tutor himself slumped back comfortably in his chair. A black man, just like all the others.

'Thank you, Willy,' he said. 'I gonna talk to this here Jan by m'self.'

'You be all right . . . '

'Sure will. Jus leave a man outside so's I can give a shout needs be.'

When the door had closed the man rose to shake hands with Jan. He was middle-aged with a full beard and long hair, both shot through with grey. His clothing was dark and conservative, well suited to the clerical dog collar.

'I'm Reverend Montour, Mr Kulozik. It is my very great pleasure to welcome you here.'

Jan shook his hand and could only nod his thanks. All traces of patois had vanished and the Reverend spoke with an easy and cultivated voice.

'Sit down, please do. May I offer you a glass of sherry. It's a local wine and I think that you will find it enjoyable.'

Jan sipped the sherry; it was quite good, and looked around the room.

'You'll pardon me for staring,' he said. 'But it's been years since I have been in a room like this. I admire your library.'

'Thank you. Most of the volumes are centuries old and quite rare. Every page has been absorbtion preserved.'

'Wrecker books, really? May I? Thank you.' He put his glass down and stepped up to the shelves. The bindings were worn and heavily repaired, and many of the titles obliterated. Reaching up he took down what looked like the soundest one and opened it carefully to the title page. It was entitled 'THE MIDDLE AGES 395 – 1500'. He turned the page carefully and on the back it read 'Copyright, 1942'.

When he spoke he had trouble keeping the reverence out of his voice. 'This book ... it's over five hundred years old. I didn't know anything like this existed.'

'They do, I assure you, and there are many more like it. But I can understand your feelings. You are British, I take it?'

Jan nodded.

'I thought so. The accent and that term, the Wreckers. I understand it is in common usage in your country. You must understand that I have these books because of the varying paths that were followed during the period that historians call the Retrocession. At that time the different countries and areas of the world suffered the same declining fate, but they accommodated to it in different ways, usually following the existing social divisions. Great Britain, traditionaly a class-orientated society, utilized its historical class system to consolidate the rigid societal structure that still exists today. The ruling élite had never been happy with education for the masses and were only too relieved when physical circumstances did away with that necessity. But restriction of education and information, once begun, has no end. I understand that most British citizens today have no idea of the true nature of history or even of the world they live in. Is that true?'

'Very much so. My accidental discovery of this fact was the beginning of a chain of events that, well, brought me to this room.'

'I understand. Conformity must be most intellectually oppressive under a system such as yours. History followed a completly different course here since there are many roads to tyranny. America, without a class system, has traditionally substituted a system of vertical mobility based for the most part on money. It was always a truism here that it was not your lineage but your bank account that determined your status. With the exception, of course, of the physically visible minorities. Irish, Polish, Jews, traditionally rejected minorities, were assimiliated after the first few generations because their racial types permitted them to merge with the general population. Not so the dark-skinned races who, once firmly planted at the bottom of society, were forced to stay there by the repeated cycles of physical and educational deprivation. This was the situation existing when the Retrocession began and it ended with this country as you see it now.'

He reached for the sherry decanter. 'Your glass is empty; I'm afraid that I am being a bad host.'

'Yes, please, not too much. And do go on. I have been for years on a planet that must be the cultural wasteland of the universe. Your words, conversation like this, you can't understand how I feel ...'

'I think I do. I know I felt the same way myself when I opened my first book. It was that same thirst for knowledge that led me to this room, to the position that I have today. I wanted to know just why the world was the way it was. I had good reason to hate it – but I also wanted to understand it. As I said, the Retrocession just increased the traditional divisions. Your police state in Britain came about through an excess of kindness, an attempt to see that everyone had at least the minimum needed for existence, the food to stay alive if nothing else. But once the state controls everything, why the men who control the state have absolute power. They do not relinquish it easily as I imagine you have found out. A completely different course was followed here. The American tradition has been to declare that the needy are really slackers and that the unemployed are that way because they are naturally lazy. The Retrocession saw the complete victory of *laissez faire*, which is simply institutionalized selfishness carried to the extreme. It is amazing the nonsense that people will believe when it is in their own interest. There were actually adherents then of an intellectually bankrupt theory called monetarism, which enabled the rich to get richer, the poor to get poorer, by applying a completely disproven economic theory in place of intelligence.'

Montour sighed at the thought, then sipped a little of his sherry.

'So the obvious happened. When the food and energy began to run out the rich first kept most of it, then all of it. After all, this had always been national policy during the years leading up to the collapse when America consumed most of the world's petroleum, caring nothing for other countries' needs. So who can blame individuals for following the same course? Any country that permits its citizens to die for want of medical attention simply because they cannot afford it, becomes a nation in moral trouble. There were riots, killing, and more riots. Guns and weapons were everywhere and they still are. The end product was a nation divided, with the browns and the blacks living as you see them, in ghettos surrounded by barbed wire. Here they grow a certain amount of food on their own, or go out to earn a bit by labouring at the menial jobs that have not been mechanized. They die in infancy or live brutally short lives. The benefits of technological society do not trickle down to them at all. Unlike your country there is no attempt to conceal the history of their physical status from them. The oppressors want the oppressed to know just what happened to them. So they will not be so foolish as to try it all over again some day. So – do you wonder at our interest in this rebellion of the planets? We look forward to it spreading to Earth.'

Jan could only nod and agree.

'Please excuse my rudeness for asking, but I don't understand why the ruling powers permitted your education.'

Montour smiled. 'They didn't. My people originally came to this country as slaves. Completely without education, torn from their roots and culture. What we have achieved since that time was done despite the position our masters had placed us in. When the breakdown began we had no intention of giving up what we had so painfully achieved. We matured as a people even as we were being oppressed as a people. If they took away everything except our intelligence – why then we would have to rely on our intelligence alone. In doing this we had the opportunity to emulate the example of another oppressed minority. The Jews. For millennia they kept their culture and their traditions alive through religion and respect for learning. The religious man, the educated man was the honoured man. We had our religion, and we had our professors and educators. Under the pressure of circumstance the two became amalgamated. The brightest boys are now honoured by being permitted to enter the ministry when they come of age. My formative years were spent in those streets. I speak the ghetto language that has developed since we were cut off from the mainstream of life. But I have learned the language of the oppressor as well as part of my education. If salvation does not come in my generation I shall pass on my wisdom to those who follow after me. But I know – I have faith – that it will come some day.'

Jan drained the last of the sherry and put the glass down, waving away the offer of more. The rapid passage of events had left him dazed; his mind was almost as tired as his body, his thoughts turning around and around. What crippled lives people were forced to lead. The proles in Britain were at least fed and protected like cattle – as long as they accepted this cattle-like role. While the people here in the black ghettos of America had no such comforts, they did at least know who they were and what they were. But along with this knowledge was the fact that they were forced to live in a state of constant rebellion.

'I really don't know which system is the worse to live under,' Jan said. 'Yours or mine.'

'No system of oppression should be condoned. And there are far worse ones in the world. The great socialist experiment in the Soviet Union was always hampered by the Czarist heritage with its obscene bits of madness like internal passports and labour camps. Whether the state there would have withered away in the end as Marx predicted we will never know. By the time of the Retrocession they still had not industrialized their basically peasant economy. It was an easy slide back to an almost feudal culture. Many died, but many have always died in Russia. The commissars and upper echelon party leaders took the place of the nobility. The titles might be different today, but any of the Czars transported ahead in time would feel right at home there now.'

'The rebellion must spread to Earth,' Jan said.

'I agree completely. We must work for that day . . . '

The door was suddenly flung open and Willy stood there, gasping for breath, a gun in each hand.

'Trouble,' he said. 'Bad trouble. Worst I ever seen.'

# Chapter Nine

'What happining?' Montour asked, shifting his speech quickly into the demotic.

'Dey's all around. More of the bolly dogs I never seen. Right around New Watts, shooting at anything moves. Wid big heat guns to burn dere way in . . . '

His words were interrupted by the distant roar of fusion cannon, overlaid with the sharp crackling of gunfire. It was loud, close by. A hard knot of fear formed in Jan's middle and he looked up and saw both men were looking at him.

'It's me they want,' he said. Reverend Montour nodded.

'Very possibly. I can't remember the last time they raided in strength like this.'

'There's no point in running any longer. Those fusion guns will burn these old buildings flat. I'm going to give myself up.'

Montour shook his head. 'We have places where you can hide. They put the fires out as they advance. They just use the guns to burn their way in.'

'I'm sorry. No. I've seen too many people killed recently. I can't be responsible for any more deaths. I'm going out to them. I will not change my mind.'

Montour stood for a moment, then nodded. 'You are a brave man. I wish we could have done more for you.' He turned to Willy. 'Leave dem guns here and show this gen'mum where the bolly dogs at.'

The two pistols thudded to the floor. Jan took the scholar's hand. 'I'll not forget you,' he said.

'Nor I, you.' Montour took a spotless white handkerchief from his breast pocket. 'Better take this. They tend to fire first.'

Willy led the way, muttering angrily to himself, through passageways and connecting buildings. They had to move aside as two gunmen ran by, dragging a third man whose clothes were soaked with blood. No end, Jan thought, no end ever.

'Fuckin' bolly dogs jes out dere,' Willy said, pointing to a door, then turned and hurried back the way they had come.

Jan shook out the folds of the handkerchief and stood to one side of the door as he eased it open. a burst of rocket slugs tore through it, screaming away down the hallway behind him.

'Stop shooting! he called out, waving the white cloth through the gap. 'I'm coming out.'

A shrill whistle blew and the sound of firing began to die away. An amplified voice called out. 'Open the door slowly. Come out, one at a time. Hands on your head. If your hands aren't there, if I see more than one man, I'm going to fire. All right – now.'

Jan laced his fingers together on top of his head and eased the door open with his toe. Then walked slowly forward to face the ranked police officers. They were impersonal as robots behind their riot masks and shields; every weapon was pointed at him.

'I'm all alone,' he said.

'That's him!' somebody called out.

'Silence,' the sergeant commanded. He holstered his weapon and waved Jan to him. 'Nice and easy, that's the way. Everson, get the car up here.'

He seized Jan's right arm with a practised motion, pulling it down behind his back to lock the handcuffs to his wrist. Then the cuffs on his other wrist. His fingers dug deep into Jan's arm as he pulled him forward.

The blackened ground was still warm as they walked through the gap in the wire to the waiting patrol car. The sergeant held Jan's head down as he pushed him into the back, then climbed in after him. There was the scream of rubber as the driver gunned the vehicle forward.

They rode in silence. Jan was defeated, empty even of words, knowing full well what was in store. Since he came originally from Earth, Security was sure to think him one of the leaders of the rebellion. They would take his mind apart looking for evidence. He knew what men looked like after treatment like that. Death would be a release.

As the car drew up before an official building the door was pulled open; the sergeant pushed Jan through it. A uniformed officer held each arm securely as he was hurried through the entrance and into a waiting elevator. Jan was too emotionally exhausted to notice or care where they were going. There had been too much killing, running. It was over at last. They dragged him into a room, slammed him into the chair. The door opposite him opened slowly and he looked at it with dull and unseeing eyes.

Thurgood-Smythe came in.

All of the fatigue, the despair, everything was washed away by a red surge of hatred.

'You've led us quite a chase, brother-in-law,' Thurgood-Smythe said. 'Now if you will promise to behave yourself I'll have those handcuffs taken off. You and I must have a serious talk.'

Jan had his head down, eyes lowered, shaking with rage, his throat too tight to speak. He nodded. 'Good,' Thurgood-Smythe said, mistaking the emotion for fear. 'I won't hurt you, you can take my word for that.'

The cuffs clicked free and Jan rubbed the marks on his

wrists, listening as heavy footsteps receded. But he could wait no longer. a harsh sound was torn from his throat as he hurled himself at his tormentor. Their bodies crashed together, Thurgood-Smythe went over and down with Jan straddling him, his arched fingers reaching for his throat. But Thurgood-Smythe had seized his wrists and was holding him at bay. Jan leaned his weight forward, pressing down, his nails clawing into Thurgood-Smythe's face, his thumbs sinking into the sockets of his eyes. Thurgood-Smythe cried out hoarsely – just as hands grabbed at Jan's shoulders, a foot thudded into the side of his neck knocking him away, other hard boots crushing into his body.

'That's enough ... ' Thurgood-Smythe said. 'Put him into the chair and get out.' He groped behind him for a chair, found it, eased into it. The gun in his hand aimed steadily at Jan. For long seconds the only sound in the room was their hoarse breathing. 'I won't have that repeated,' Thurgood-Smythe finally said. 'I have some important things to tell you, important for all of us, but I still will not hesitate to shoot you the instant you move in this direction. Do you understand.'

'I understand that you killed my friends, murdered Sara before me ... '

'What is done is done. Your mewling about it or feeling sorry for yourself will not change it ... '

'Kill me and have it over with. Your cat and mouse game doesn't interest me. When we parted you told me to work or be destroyed. I've ceased work, other than to work for the overthrow of you and people like you. Get it over with.'

'Such a rush for annihilation.' Thurgood-Smythe smiled slightly and pushed a runnel of blood from the corner of his mouth; his face was torn and bruised, blood welling from the sockets of his eyes. He ignored the pain; the gun did not move at all from its target. 'Not quite like you.'

'I've changed. You saw to that.'

'Indeed you have. And matured as well I sincerely hope. Enough to sit and listen to what I have to say. I've come a long way since last we met. Now I sit on the United Nations council and act as liaison chief between global security and space defences. The UNO itself is just a toothless debating society, since there is no shared power in this world – no matter what the propaganda in the papers says. Every country is a law unto itself. However there are committees to handle international trade agreements as well as the space program. Spaceconcent in California is a truly international, and until recently, an interplanetary organization. We both know that it is slightly reduced in size these days. Since there is little feedback between Spaceconcent and the various countries that profit from its enterprises, my position is both a secure and a powerful one. A most responsible position, as your sister keeps telling me. She is very fit, by the way, I thought you would want to know. My work is so responsible that I report to no one at all about security matters. That means I can do exactly what I want with you. Exactly.'

'Do you expect me to plead for mercy?'

'You misunderstand, Jan, please hear me out. Everything has changed in the last few months. As you know our forces have been defeated, driven from every planet that Earth settled. These are drastic times and they call for drastic measures. Therefore all charges against you have been dropped. You are a free man, Jan, with all the rights of a free citizen.'

Jan laughed. 'Do you really expect me to believe that? The next thing will be you asking me to go to work for you.'

75

'You are being prescient. I did have something like that in mind. I have a job that is perfectly suited to your background and experience.' He hesitated a moment, enjoying the drama of the occasion.

'It is quite an important job for you to undertake. I want you to contact some resistance people here on Earth. As a liaison man for me.'

Jan shook his head slowly. 'Do you really think that I would betray them to you? What a sick creature you are.'

'My dear Jan, I can understand your attitude, it is a reasonable one under the circumstances. But hear me out, please. I am going to tell you things about myself that you have never known or suspected. Remember, we were friends once. Perhaps we can be so again after you hear what I have to say. Like you, as a young man, I became intrigued about the world and how it was run. Since I had no resources other than my ambition I knew I would have to make my own way. Like you I became disgusted when I discovered the sort of lives we were leading. Unlike you, I joined the forces of oppression rather than attempt to fight them. So that I could burrow from within, you might say ...'

'Sorry, you dirty son of a bitch, but it won't wash. I've seen you at your work, seen how you enjoy it.'

'I am rather good, aren't I? But it is all protective colouration. I saw that Security was the real force in control of the world – so I determined to run Security. To do this I had to outdo all my rivals, to be the best at my chosen task. It was not easy but it was worth it, and I achieved two goals at the same time. I rose to power by being the most reactionary of all. No one has ever doubted me. Nor have they ever understood that by operating in this manner I was increasing oppression and therefore the forces of resistance. I am proud to feel that this policy

76

created the climate that fostered the present rebellion. Since the planets are free my work has succeeded.'

Jan shook his head. 'No, that is impossible to believe.'

'It happens to be true – but true or no it will make no difference to our relationship. From this moment on you are a free man with all the privileges that go with that status. Your criminal record has been expunged from the files and your own record returned to the computer banks. Your absence from Earth for these last years has been explained as a matter of Security. For anyone with first priority identification the record also shows that you have always been a high Security officer and that all of your other work has been a front for your operations. You are now very rich and your bank account is full. Here is your identification card. Welcome back, Jan. There's a bar here and I have had the foresight to stock it with champagne.'

It was all some kind of sadistic trick, Jan knew that. His body, his neck, ached were he had been kicked but he had no time to consider the pain, he ignored it, fought it away so that he could order his thoughts. He had to use intelligence, not raw emotion. Though he had no regrets over the anger that had hurled him at his brother-in-law; how he had enjoyed the animal pleasure of actually laying his hands on the one person that he hated the most! But what was the man up to now? This had to be a plot of some kind; Thurgood-Smythe was incapable of any straightforward action. But whatever he was planning could not be uncovered at the present moment. Should he play along? Pretend to believe him? Did he have any choice? If the identification were real then there might be a chance to escape from the Security net. So it did not matter what he said if he managed to leave this room alive. He had no compunction about lying to his brother-in-law; it was almost an obligation. Therefore it was of no importance what he promised, but what he did. Promise anything, get away to safety. That was a good deal better than the certain death that awaited him if he refused. Jan watched with unbelief as Thurgood-Smythe carefully levered the cork out of the bottle, then poured two glasses of champagne without spilling a drop. He turned and smiled as he crossed the room and handed one to Jan. Who repressed the desire to smash in that smile now that the gun had been laid aside for the moment.

'That's a good deal better,' Thurgood-Smythe said. 'Just resist the urge for violence and you will stay alive. You are not the suicidal type.'

'All right. I'll work along with you. Do what you ask. But I will betray no one, give you no information.'

'Very good. I ask no more. So we can drink to the future and hope that it will be a bright one for mankind.' He raised his glass in salute; they drank.

'What must I do?' Jan asked.

'Go on a mission for me. To Israel. Now do you see the trust and faith behind my offer? If you doubt what I say why you can defect and simply stay there – and none the wiser.'

'I can't believe that. You proved to me that you had liaison with the Israeli government, to keep track of their agents.'

'Liaison, yes. But I have no say over what happens in that sovereign state. As you will discover, they are a very strong-willed people. And now I will tell you a secret, one that is proof of my sincerity in this matter because it puts my life in your hands. Under the code name Cassius, I have been supplying the Israelis with classified Security information. They are very grateful, since I have asked nothing in return other than the knowledge that I am working for the benefit of the human race. They think very well of Cassius, so will trust you implicitly when you reveal that you are Cassius. I will give you the identification code, also a copy of all the information I have sent them in the past few years. What happens next is up to you. If you reveal this fact in the right quarters here you will find that there are any number of Security people who would love to topple me and take my place, to destroy me. Or you can go to Israel and pass on what could be the most important message you ever carried in your entire lifetime. The choice is yours, Jan.'

Choice? Jan could not believe that there was one. He was sure that any attempt to convey information to another Security officer here would only end in his instant destruction. Thurgood-Smythe was incapable of allowing a thing like that to happen. No. He had to go along with the plan. Take the message to Israel and let them decide what his brother-in-law was up to. The world was turning upside down. A portion of Thurgood-Smythe's story might be true. He might very well be deserting the sinking ship for his own benefit. Jan knew that he was out of his depth.

'All right,' he said. 'Tell me what I have to do.'

'Good man. You'll not be sorry.'

Thurgood-Smythe went to the desk and took up a thick plastic envelope. He handed it to Jan.

'I'm going to put you on a plane to New York now. You're not very safe here since everyone in California and Arizona is still on the lookout for you. But I did not let the alarm go out nationwide. A room has been booked for you at the Waldorf-Astoria. Get some rest, buy some clothes, eat a few good meals. Then, when you feel up to it open this package and memorize the basic material it contains. No need to be word perfect, you just want to be aware of everything here. It contains the security information I passed on to the Israelis. Very incriminating for me, so

79

don't leave it lying about. You'll have about eight hours to read it before the paper disintegrates. Then phone me at the number on the outside of the envelope so I can take the next step. Any questions?'

'So many that I wouldn't know where to begin. This all takes a bit of getting used to.'

'I realize. Welcome aboard, Jan. It's nice to have someone to help me, to confide in after all of the years of working alone.' He extended his hand.

Jan looked at it and, after a long moment's hesitation, shook his head.

'I can't forget that easily. There is too much blood on that hand for me to touch.'

'Aren't you being a little overdramatic?'

'Perhaps. I'll work with you since I have no choice. But that doesn't mean that I have to like it – or like you. Understood?'

Thurgood-Smythe's eyes narrowed slightly, but when he spoke there was no anger in his voice.

'Whatever you say, Jan. Success is more important than our personal feelings. It's time for you to leave now.'

# Chapter Ten

During the night the thudding of distant explosions had woken Jan. He had clearly heard them here, on the thirtieth floor, despite the soundproofing and the double glazed windows. He had opened the door and stepped onto the balcony outside. Something was burning brightly across the city. Sirens and warblers wailed as police and fire equipment tore by in the streets below. The fire burned for a long time. It was muggy and hot outside of the airconditioned room and he did not watch long. He was still tired and fell asleep again as soon as he was back in bed.

Bright sunshine poured through the windows in the morning when he touched the button to open the curtains. An apparently original Rembrandt painting hanging on the far wall became a screen, as he switched the television on. Jan scanned the news headlines, punched for LOCAL NEWS then brought up EXPLOSION AND FIRE. The list vanished and was replaced by a scene centred around a park bench. There was green grass and trees behind the bench, while a few pigeons pecked at the path before it. A man and a woman sat at opposite ends of the bench, both radiant and healthy, good looking and suntanned. All over, for they were both nude. They smiled at him with glowing white teeth. 'Good morning,' the man said. 'I'm Kevin O'Donnell.'

'And I'm Patti Pierce. Would you like me or Kevin to bring you the news today?'

Then they waited, frozen and unmoving, the pigeons

motionless as well, even the breeze-tossed leaves were still. The computer control waited for him to decide.

'Patti, of course,' Jan said, and the camera moved in slowly on the girl who stood and smiled in his direction. Whether she was real or only a program in the computer was unimportant. She was both beautiful and desirable and certainly made the news more interesting. Though he could not understand what nude announcers had to do with the news.

'The Apple was busy last night,' Patti said, standing and pointing over her shoulder. The park vanished to be replaced by a burning building, flames billowing high against the black sky. Fire equipment was drawn up in the street before it and men with hoses were fighting the blaze. Patti, rotating her behind sweetly, walked over and climbed into the driver's seat of a hook and ladder.

'This warehouse caught fire in the early hours and burned like a house on fire, yes sir! Four companies were called out and it took until dawn to damp down the blaze and keep it from spreading. Paint and chemicals had been stored in the building which kept things mighty hot for our helmeted heroes, yes sir! No one as yet knows how the blaze started, but arson has definitely been ruled out.'

One of the helmeted heroes ran up and unclipped a piece of equipment from the truck near Patti. He never noticed her. The computer simulation was perfect; she could really have been at the fire rather than recording in the studio.

Someone knocked on the door. Jan turned off the TV and smiled at himself for feeling guilty; everyone else would be watching the nude news announcers as well. 'Come in,' he called out, and the door unlocked.

'Good morning, sir, lovely morning,' the waiter said, carrying in Jan's breakfast on a tray. He was young, white, and slightly adenoidal; a whispy moustache struggled for existence on his upper lip. He bowed as he put the tray down on the bedside table.

'That was quite a fire last night,' Jan said.

'Jigaboos done it,' the waiter answered, breathing hard through his open mouth. 'None of them come to work in the kitchen today, not one. Show's they done it.'

'You think they started the fire? The news said the cause was unknown ...'

'They always say that. It had to be the spooks. This time they oughta let Harlem burn to the ground.'

Jan was uncomfortable in the presence of the raw hatred. He poured some coffee; the waiter bowed again and left. He had never before realized how divided America was by racial barriers. It must always have been there, below the surface. War fever was bringing it out now. There was nothing he could do about it, nothing at all. He turned the news on again and watched Patti prance through the scenes while he gave his attention to the scrambled eggs and bacon.

When he got out of bed, Jan noticed the sealed envelope on the sideboard where he had dropped it. He wasn't ready to open it yet – was not even sure if he should open it. Because when he did so he knew he would have to join Thurgood-Smythe in his mad scheme. He realized suddenly that his head was fuzzy, that he had trouble coming to grips with reality. It was not surprising. The changes had been too abrupt. After the years of dull toil on Halvmörk, everything had been turned upside down. First leaving that planet on the spacer, then being captured, escaping, capture again – and finally his brother in law's revelation that everything was all going to turn out right after all. Jan was very suspicious of sudden happy endings. He went into the marble and gold luxury of the bathroom and looked at himself in the mirror. Red eyes with dark circles around them, and grey in the stubble on his chin. Whatever he decided to do next would be done in a leisurely fashion. He was not going to rush into anything for some time.

There was a circular bathtub here that was big enough to swim in. He set the temperature to warm and pressed the FILL button. It did, instantly, with a quiet rushing sound. There must be a reservoir, preheated, somewhere close by. He stepped into the tub, aware just how far he was from New Watts and the Harlem that the waiter had talked about. Aware also how close he was to them at the same time. This world where a few lived in luxury, where most existed at the brink of despair, was a precarious place. The waves of revolution from the stars were touching Earth now. Would they carry the rebellion here as well?

'I hope you like the bath,' the girl said, stepping forward to the middle of the room. She was dressed in a short terrycloth robe which she slowly took off; she was gorgeously naked underneath. When she dropped the robe it vanished – and Jan realized he was looking at a holograph projection.

'The management of the Waldorf-Astoria wants you to enjoy the best in comforts during your stay. If you wish I can massage your back while you are relaxing in the tub, soap you and scrub you as well. Dry you and give you a more exciting massage in the bed. Would you like that, Sir.'

Jan shook his head, then realized that the frozen hologram image was waiting for a verbal instruction.

'No. Get thee behind me, Satan.' The girl vanished. Jan's wife was light years away, yet she was very close still in his emotions. He finished soaping and washing and when he stepped out of the tub the water vanished behind him in a single mighty insufflation.

When he had arrived the day before no eyebrows had

been raised nor any attention paid to his sleezy clothes or lack of luggage. Not when he was occupying one of the best suites in the hotel. But he would need new clothes; that was the first order of business. He dressed quickly and kicked into the sandals. There was a safe set into the wall of the sitting room and he put Thurgood-Smythe's envelope in it; keying in a new combination so that only he could open it. With his ID card in his shirt pocket he would have everything he needed. He patted the card and went out.

The lobby of the hotel was filled with elegantly dressed guests, mostly women, who were strolling towards the doors leading to a fashion show. Jan felt decidedly scruffy as he pushed through them and out into the soggy heat of the day. When he had arrived the previous evening he had noticed that there were a number of shops along Lexington Avenue. Clothes, shoes, luggage – there was everything here that he might need.

Though some vehicles were passing there seemed to be few pedestrians. None at all he realized, just as a policeman stepped out of a doorway and stopped him by pushing his nightstick hard into Jan's chest.

'All right, stupid. You want trouble you got trouble.'

Jan's temper flared; he had seen enough of the police in the last twenty-four hours.

'I'm afraid that you are the one who is in trouble, officer.' He took out his ID. 'You will look at this and then you will apologize for your brutal manner.'

The policeman let the stick drop slowly. Jan's refined accent and manner did not match his clothing. When he saw the Security symbol next to the three digit number indicating Jan's rank he actually began to tremble. He saluted and Jan felt ashamed of himself for bullying the man with his newly attained rank and position. His actions, in essence, were really the same as those of the police officers who had raided New Watts.

'I didn't know, I'm sorry, but the things that you're wearing...'

'I understand,' Jan said, putting the card back into his pocket. 'It was an emergency. I'm going to buy new clothes now.'

'I'll show you, sir, just follow me. I'll wait to take you back. You don't want to be on the streets today.'

'Is there an alert?'

'No. But people know. The word goes around. We shot the two guys what burned down the armoury. Both white. What the fuck did they think they was doing? In here. Best place on Madison. I'll be outside.' He hammered loudly on the sealed door with his nightstick and it was quickly unlocked. 'Take good care of this gentleman,' he told the wide-eyed clerk, spinning the stick swiftly on the end of its thong.

It was a gentlemen's outfitters, very exclusive, very expensive. Jan took a great deal of pleasure in spending a large amount of his newly acquired money. Shirts, slacks, undergarments, suits, everything lightweight, easily packed and uncrushable. If it was hot in New York – Israel was sure to be an oven. He did not mind heat, but he liked to be dressed for it. Shoes and a better grade of sandal than he was wearing completed his outfit. His image in the mirror was greatly improved.

'Send the rest to the Waldorf,' he said, passing over his card. He pointed to his discarded clothing. 'And dispose of these.'

'Very good, sir. If you would please approve the sales slip..?' Jan waved it away; it wasn't his own money being spent. The clerk slipped Jan's ID into the machine, entered the sum to be debited, then returned the card. The money had been transferred from Jan's account to that of the shop's.

The waiting policeman nodded approvingly at Jan's new clothing. The world was in order again. He led the way to a luggage shop, then found an optician where Jan could get some sunglasses; he was not used to the glare of full daylight after his years on the twilight world. On impulse he bought a second pair and handed them to the policeman when he came out. The man gaped, then slowly put them on. Pulling in his stomach as he looked at his image in a shopwindow.

'I ain't gonna forget this, sir. You're a right guy. I never met a Limey before, but I think you're right guys.'

There were a few more pedestrians about now and the officer looked closely at each one as they passed. His nightstick spun faster as a black man in ragged clothing came towards them. The man kept his eyes lowered and touched a large plastic badge on his shirt as he went by; identification of some sort. Very suddenly Jan had had enough of the city and was happy to be off the street and in the cool seclusion of the hotel. The keyboy led the way to the elevator, then unlocked the door to the suite for him.

His purchases had been delivered and were waiting in a neat row of boxes in the lounge. He looked from them to the decorated door of the safe. The moment could be put off no longer. It was time to find out what he was getting into. When he pulled the tab on Thurgood-Smythe's envelope there was a brief hiss as the air entered it. Inside was a thin file of papers. He sat down and began to read.

It was a chronicle of evil covering the past two years. Each parcel of information was dated, each statement brief and to the point. People arrested and imprisoned, people killed. Foreign agents detected and their movements chronicled, intelligence supplied by British agents and embassies. There were interesting titbits of information that surely had never appeared in the news. The Lord Mayor of London, a prominent wholesaler, had apparently been deeply involved in the black market for food. Security knew this but did nothing – until they observed that some German agents had uncovered the fact as well and had used it to blackmail the man. Murder, or rather a fatal accident, had eliminated the problem. There was more like this. Jan scanned quickly through the pages, then went back and memorized the names and dates of the most important events. It was boring but necessary work. After a few hours of it he realized that he was hungry and phoned down to room service. The menu was extensive and far more interesting than anything he had eaten in the past years. He ordered a broiled lobster and a chilled bottle of Louis Martini sauterne and kept on reading.

Later, when he was turning over a sheet, the corner broke off in his hand. He quickly riffled through the stack to be sure that he could recall as much as he had need of. There were fragments of paper and ink on his hands now and he went into the bathroom to wash them off. When he came out the sheets of paper had turned into a pile of gray dust.

Jan picked up the envelope and looked at the telephone number on it. Thurgood-Smythe's number. Had he any choice?

The answer was still *no*. This entire matter might be some devious plan of his brother-in-law's, undoubtedly was. There was still nothing he could do about it. If he did not cooperate he was sure that his new status would be stripped from him as quickly as it had been bestowed. He would go along with the scheme, get out of the country – then reassess it when he was safe.

He punched the number into the phone and sat back. Seconds later Thurgood-Smythe's grim features appeared on the screen. He smiled slightly when he saw who it was.

'Well, Jan, enjoying your stay in New York, I trust?'

'I've read the papers.'

'Very good. And your decision . . . ?'

'I'll go along with your plan until I learn different. You knew that all the time.'

'Of course. Welcome aboard. If you will send for a taxi in about an hour you will be just on time for a specially chartered flight to Cairo. It is full of technicians and engineers for the reopened oil fields. Since you have been away the thermal extraction technique has succeeded in pumping petroleum from these depleted fields for the first time in four centuries. You will be joining them as a specialist in micro-electronic circuitry, which of course you are. Tickets, passport and a new ID card are waiting for you at the porter's desk. Keep your present ID for emergencies. Your new ID has another function as well. Your file number is also Cassius's identification code. When this number is divided by the day of the month, all of the digits to the left of the decimal point are the code for that day.'

'So I go to Cairo. Then what?'

'You will be contacted. Enjoy your trip. And make a note of this number for later use. With it you can contact me instantly, wherever I am. Good-bye.'

Jan had just enough time to pack his bags leisurely before ringing down to the desk. He wondered where it would all end. He had a certain amount of trepidation about setting his foot on this road when he had no idea of where it might lead. Yet he was not sorry to be leaving the United States.

# Chapter Eleven

For six full days, Jan lost himself in his work. The petroleum wells in the Sinai desert were the first installation to make use of the highly complex thermal extraction technique. But it was like working in the cemetery of a forgotten age, because their camp was in the centre of the played-out oil fields. Ancient pumps and drilling towers stretched away on all sides, silent and still, preserved through the past centuries by the arid desert. The modern installation was as new and bright an a freshly minted coin, standing out in stark contrast to the desolation on all sides. The buildings were prefabricated and glossy, as was all of the equipment. Their techniques were new and original as well, but very prone to develop operational bugs. Karaman, the petrologist, sat in the laboratory swirling a dark and tarry liquid about in a glass flask.

'It is good, very good – but pumping has stopped again, the third time in as many days,' he said. 'Why?'

'Feedback controls,' Jan said. 'You've been on this project longer than I have so you know the problems. There is a little bit of white-hot hell that we have created down there in the sand. First the nitrogen is pumped down and converted to a plasma by the fusion generator. That in turn heats the sand and rock which evaporates some of the volatiles which in turn creates pressure which pushes that petroleum to the surface. That's the theory. But in practice there are about a hundred different things that can go wrong with the process ...'

'I know. Everything from blowing the whole thing up or setting fire to it, or even melting down the reactor which happened to us once in California. But, honestly Jan, we're years past that stage.'

'But you are not years past monitoring inputs. There just aren't enough of them to keep accurate watch on the process. It begins to cycle and the cycles build and get out of control, so you have to shut down and go back to the beginning and start over again. But we have some new learning software that is beginning to predict the cycles and stop them before they happen. You have to give it a chance.'

Karaman swirled the oil around gloomily, then put the jar down to answer the phone. 'It's the director,' he said. 'Wants you in his office soonest.'

'Right.'

The director held out a communication to Jan when he came through the door. 'Something big coming apart at the central office. They need you, they say, yesterday or earlier. I have no idea what it is about except the bastards could not have picked a worse time to pull you out. We're finally getting the production levelled and on line. Tell them that, will you. They don't seem to listen to me any more. Make them happy and grab the next plane back here. A pleasure to have you on the site, Kulozik. There's a cab here to pick you up.'

'I'll have to pack . . . '

'Don't worry. I took the liberty of having the BOQ servant put all your stuff into your bags. Get moving, so you can get back.'

Jan had more than a suspicion that he was not on his way to Suez and Cairo. The Arab cabdriver put Jan's bags into the back then salaamed respectfully as he held the door open for him. It was cool in the air-conditioned interior, after the walk from the buildings. As they pulled away from the installation the driver took a flat metal box from the seat and passed it back to him.

'Lift the lid, sir, and a push button lock is revealed. If you are not aware of the combination do not experiment in cab, I beg you. Explosions follows error.'

'Thanks,' Jan said, weighing the package in his hands. 'Is there anything else?'

'A meeting. I am taking you to the place of assignation. There is, I regret, a payment of eighty pounds for this service.'

Jan was sure that the man had been well paid for this service and that this additional payment was a little bit of free enterprise. He passed the money over in any case. His bank balance was still unbelievable. They drove down the smooth highway for a half an hour – then turned sharply into one of the unmarked tracks that led out into the desert. A short while later they came to the scene of some forgotten battlefield filled with the shells of wrecked tanks and disabled field guns.

'Here please,' the driver said, opening the door. Heat pressed in in a savage wave. Jan got out and looked around. There was nothing in sight except the empty desert and the burned wreckage. When he turned back he saw that his bags were on the sand and the driver was climbing back into the cab.

'Hold it!' Jan called put. 'What happens next?'

The man did not answer. Instead he gunned the engine to life, spun the vehicle in a tight circle and sped back towards the highway. The dust of his passage swirled over Jan who cursed fluently while he wiped his dripping face with the back of his hand.

When the sound of the cab died away the silence and the loneliness pressed in. It was very peaceful, but a little frightening at the same time. And hot, searingly hot. If he had to walk back to the highway he would have to leave his bags here. He wouldn't want to carry them, not in this temperature. He laid the metal box in the shade of the bags and hoped the explosive it contained was not heat sensitive.

'You are Cassius?' the voice said.

Jan turned about, startled, since he had not heard any footsteps in the muffling sand. The girl stood there, near the ruined tank, and the arrow of memory startled him so that he almost spoke her name aloud. No, Sara was dead, killed years ago. Yet the first glimpse of this suntanned girl in the brief khaki shorts, with her blonde, shoulder-length hair, had startled him. The resemblance was so close. Or was his memory betraying him after all the years? She was an Israeli like Sara, that was all. He realized that he was still staring in silence and had not answered her.

'I'm from Cassius, yes. My name is Jan.'

'Dvora,' she said stepping forward and taking his hand; her grip was firm, warm. 'We have long suspected that Cassius was more than one person. But we can talk about that later, out of this sun. Can I help you with your bags?'

'I think I can manage. There is transportation?'

'Yes, out of sight of the road behind this wreck.'

It was the same sort of vehicle they used in the oil camp, a half-track, with wheels at the front and tractor treads behind. Jan threw his bags into the back and climbed up into the high front seat next to Dvora. There were no doors. It was open at the sides for air, but a solid metal roof kept the sun off them. Dvora threw a switch on the steering column and they started forward silently, with only the slightest hum coming from the wheels.

'Electric?' Jan asked.

She nodded and pointed at the floor. 'High density batteries under the floor, about four hundred kilos of them. But out here these vehicles are almost self-sufficient. The roof is covered with macroyield solar cells, a new development. If you don't put too many K's on this thing during the day it will stay recharged without being plugged to the mains.' She turned her head and frowned slightly when she found him staring at her again.

'Please excuse me,' Jan said. 'I know I'm being rude looking at you like that. But you remind me of someone I knew, a good many years ago. She was also an Israeli like you.'

'Then you have been to our country before?'

'No. This is the first time. We met near here and I saw her again in England.'

'You're lucky. Very few of our people get to travel at all.'

'She was – how shall I say – a very talented person. Her name was Sara.'

'Very common, like all of the biblical names.'

'Yes, I'm sure so. I heard her last name just once. Giladi. Sara Giladi.'

Dvora reached down and switched off the wheel motors. The half-track clanked jerkily to a stop. Then she half turned on the seat to face Jan, her face impassive, her large dark eyes staring into his.

'There are no coincidences in this world, Jan. Now I know why they sent me instead of one of the musclebound field agents. My name is Giladi as well. Sara was my sister.'

She was, she had to be. So much of Sara was in the turn of her cheek, her voice, reminding him constantly of the girl he had once known.

'Sara is dead,' Dvora said quietly. 'Did you know that?'

His smile was twisted, humourless. 'I was there when she was killed. We were together. Trying to get out of England. And there was no need for it, stupid, she shouldn't have died. It was a terrible, terrible waste.'

Memory flooded back, the guns, the murder. And

Thurgood-Smythe's presence. All done under his command. Jan's jaw was locked tight as he remembered and Dvora saw his fingers clench onto the grab handle.

'They told me nothing, no details,' Dvora said. 'Just that she had died in the service. You . . . you were in love with her?'

'Is it that obvious?'

'It is to me. I loved her too. Can you tell me what happened.'

'Of course. It's simple enough. We were trying to leave the country, but we never had a chance. We were betrayed from the very beginning. But she didn't know that. Instead of surrendering she fired at them, made them shoot back, willing herself to die so they could not have her knowledge. And that is the most terrible part. They had known everything all of the time.'

'I didn't hear anything about that. It is terrible, even more terrible for you because you are alive to remember it.'

'It is, yes, but I suppose that it is all past history. We can't bring her back.'

That was what he said. But he was silent about the rest of his thoughts as the half-track started up again. Perhaps Thurgood-Smythe and Security had physically killed her. But she had been betrayed by her own people, by her own organization right here in Israel. At least that is what Thurgood-Smythe had said. Where was the truth? He was going to try and find that out before he had anything more to do with these people.

It was a gruelling drive and they had little to say to each other, locked in their own thoughts. The sand gave way to rock, then sand again, then to low hills. Road signs in Hebrew began to appear and he realized that they were out of the Sinai and in Israel.

'Is it much further?'

95

'A half an hour, no more. We are going to Beersheba. He is waiting for you there?'

'Who?'

Her silence was an answer, and they drove on in the same silence after that. On a paved road now, through small, dusty villages and irrigated fields. Suddenly the desert was gone and everything was green. Across a valley a small city appeared ahead, but they turned off before they reached it. Up a narrow winding road to a solitary villa surrounded by jacaranda trees.

'Leave your bags,' Dvora said, climbing down and stretching. 'They'll be taken care of. But bring the metal box. He's expecting that.'

Two young men came out as they entered, waving to Dvora as they passed. Jan followed her through the cool house to a balcony overlooking the valley and the city beyond. An old man, grey haired and rail thin, easily in his eighties, came forward to meet them.

'Shalom, Jan Kulozik,' he said in a strong voice, its richness unexpected in a man his age. 'I am Amri Ben-Haim. Please sit down.'

'Then sending Dvora to meet me was no coincidence?'

'No, of course not.'

'Then some explanations are in order,' Jan said. Still standing.

'Yes they are. And I imagine you would like to discuss that part of the affair first.'

'I want Dvora to hear it.'

'That is understood, the why she is here. Now we sit down?'

Jan relented and dropped into one of the cane chairs. There was cold lemonade in a jug on the table and he gratefully accepted a large glass of it. He drained it quickly and it was refilled for him. He sat tensely, the bomb-protected metal box on his lap. He would turn it over to them, but wanted to hear what Ben-Haim had to say first.

'Do you know who Thurgood-Smythe is?' Jan asked.

Amri Ben-Haim nodded. 'The former head of British Security. He has climbed still higher in the last few years and is now perhaps the top Security officer in the world. His position might even be stronger than that. We know that he is directly involved with military liaison with the United Nations.'

'Did you know that he is my brother-in-law? That he is the one who trapped me and Sara – and saw her shot?'

'I am aware of all those things, yes.'

And now the important question. Jan carefully set his glass on the table and tried to relax. Nevertheless his next words had a sharp edge to them.

'Thurgood-Smythe was apparently aware of the London resistance movement from the very beginning. He had it penetrated and watched, and arrested its members when it suited him. He also knew that Sara was an Israeli, a secret she died to keep because she was sure this country would suffer if her nationality was known. Her sacrifice was needless because not only did he know about her, but he claimed to be working with your government here. He said that you identified any Israelis who tried to work on their own outside this country. Is that true?'

'Yes and no,' Amri Ben-Haim said.

'That's not much of an answer.'

'I will attempt to explain. This nation has a dubious relationship with the large power blocs who operate under the name of the United Nations. During the Retrocession they completly forgot the Near East. Once the oil wells ran dry they were happy to turn their backs on this troublesome part of the world. Free of outside interference Israel finally could make peace here. There was war, of course, as soon as the major countries went away. We died, by the thousands but we survived. The Arab governments very quickly used up their imported weapons and were naturally enough not resupplied. Defeated here they fell back upon tradition and squabbled and fought among themselves as they had always done. A jehad, a holy war, spread from Iran and swept up to our borders. We survived that as well. Hunger finally replaced their consuming interest in religion and people began to starve and die of disease. That is where we helped. Unlike the world powers we have never attempted to impose a western-orientated, machine intensive and high consumption society on this part of the world. It does not suit the local conditions. What we have done is to develop and improve on the ancient agricultural techniques, while introducing suitable technological processes, such as desalination of water, that have important applications in the area.'

'Aren't you straying from my question?'

'Please indulge me a moment longer, Jan Kulozik. Everything that I say is relevant. We cultivated our back garden you might say. Encouraged food and light manufacturing suitable to this part of the world, cured disease and built hospitals, trained doctors. Nor did we forget our own defence. We made peace on all sides, since peace is the best form of security. I don't think you realize what that means, historically speaking. The oldest written records, including the Old Testament of the Bible, are records of warfare. Unending warfare. It is over now. So when a measure of stability returned and other nations once again became aware of the Near East it was settled and peaceful and ready to supply them with year round supplies of agricultural products. I won't say that they exactly fell into our arms with happiness, in fact a few overtures were made for more direct control. This was when our atomic missiles, most of them located outside of Israel, became important. We will never start an atomic war, if for no other reason other than the inescapable fact that we are small enough to be eliminated by a few well placed hydrogen bombs. But the others know that even when dead we would fight back. The price for an atomic war then became such a high one that no country in the world was willing to pay it. So an arrangement was worked out, which has continued happily for hundreds of years. We stay in and they stay out. It means that we Jews, at one time the most cosmopolitan peoples in the world, have become the most insular. Of course in order to maintain this carefully balanced relationship we do have governmental liaison at a high level. We also rely a good deal on intelligence agents.'

'Spies?'

'Another word for them. The other countries have theirs too. We know because we capture them regularly. Unfortunately they capture some of ours as well. To return to your question. By the time we discovered that Sara's cover had been penetrated it was effectively too late to do anything to help her . . . '

'Excuse my interrupting again, Mr Ben-Haim, but I think you are just waffling. That may be taken as an insult to a man of your age and position, but it's true. You have yet to answer my question.'

'Patience, young man,' Ben-Haim said, raising his hand palm outwards. 'I am almost there. Thurgood-Smythe told us he was going to capture Sara and wanted to exchange her for three of his own agents that we had in custody. I of course agreed. So we did know that Sara was in danger of capture, and yes, I was in contact with Thurgood-Smythe.'

'He told mè that you had informed on Sara and told him

as well of the presence of all your younger agents in Britain who were working on their own.'

'He lied to you. We never had any such arrangement. None of our agents work on their own, no matter what Thurgood-Smythe or the agents themselves have told you.'

Jan sat back, exasperated.

'Then one of you is lying,' he said.

'Exactly. Now you see why I forced you to listen to a boring history of our country's problems. So you might be able to judge who is the biggest liar. Myself – or Thurgood-Smythe.'

'You both could be. He from the most selfish of motives, you from the most noble. All I know is that Sara is dead.'

'She is,' Ben-Haim said, and the words were a sigh. 'I did not know it was going to happen and I would have done anything to prevent it. Anything else is a lie, a filthy, filthy lie.'

'And Thurgood-Smythe is the world's dirtiest liar. We are all stuck in his web. Myself in particular. I have come here as Cassius, the one who provided you with the top-secret information for the past two years.'

'Thank you, Cassius. We are most grateful.'

'If you like I can tell you all about that information, as proof of my authenticity. I memorized that information about a week ago. Would you like to know who Cassius really is?'

Ben-Haim nodded. 'Verification would help. We have been sure from the start that it could only be Thurgood-Smythe. That was why we were so intrigued when you appeared.'

'He's playing with us,' Jan said with sudden realization. 'Playing games with us all.'

'Yes,' Ben-Haim nodded, 'I am sure that is a part of it.

Though not all. He could have prepared the Cassius role for a number of reasons. But when you returned to Earth so suddenly, out of the blue so to speak, he seized upon your arrival as an opportunity not to be refused. Now we will just have to find out for ourselves what he is up to. I believe you have a package there?'

Jan put the metal box on the table.

'It has a combination lock,' he said. 'And explosives that will be detonated by the wrong combination. At least that is what a very slippery cab driver told me.'

'I am sure that you are informed correctly. I have a seven digit number given me by Cassius when this affair began. Could that be the combination?'

'I don't know.' Jan stared at the smooth case. 'I have no idea what the combination is.'

'Then we will have to try mine.' Ben-Haim reached for the box, but Dvora leaned over and took it first.

'I don't feel it is wise for all of us to sit here while the lock is tried. We want a volunteer. Me. Could I have the number please, Amri Ben-Haim?'

'Get someone else,' Jan said, quickly. 'I'll do it.'

'There is already a volunteer,' Ben-Haim said as he passed a slip of paper over to the girl. She took this and the case and went down the steps into the garden, walking to the far end by the wall. When she reached it she turned to wave to them, then turned back and bent over the sealed metal box.

# Chapter Twelve

Jan felt the tension drain from him when she straightened up and held the box over her head.

'There was little danger,' Ben-Haim said. 'Or I wouldn't have sent her – and you wouldn't have let her go.'

Dvora ran up the stairs, smiling and breathless, and laid the open case on the table. Ben-Haim reached in and took out a flat rectangle of black plastic.

'A Mark fourteen hard disc memory,' Jan said. 'Where is your terminal?'

'Inside. I will take you there,' Ben-Haim said, leading the way. Dvora stood aside to let Jan by and on sudden impulse he took her hands in his.

'That was a foolish thing to do . . . '

'No it wasn't and you knew that. And besides, it will look good on my service record.'

She was laughing, only half serious, and Jan's laugh echoed hers. Only then did he realize that he was still holding her hands; he tried to pull away but Dvora held them firmly. The same impulse had seized her and before she released her grip she leaned out and kissed him. Her eyes were open, dark, her lips moist and warm. He returned the kiss and this time it was she who dropped his hands. She stepped back and after a long and expressive look she turned and led the way into the house. Ben-Haim was standing in front of the computer terminal tapping the buttons.

'No success,' he said. 'It keeps asking for a code reference before it will run. I have no idea what it means.'

Jan leaned over and looked at the letters on the screen.

ENTER CORRECT ACCESS CODE
NOW – ENTERING INCORRECT
CODE WILL WIPE THE MEMORY

'And you have no idea what the code is?' Jan said, mostly to himself. 'Then if you don't have it – I must. And I can think of only one thing.' He took out his new ID card and looked at the number. 'Thurgood-Smythe told me that this number was Cassius's identification code when divided by the day of the month. But you never asked me for an identifying code?'

'We had no reason to – or instructions.'

'Then this must be it.'

Jan fed the number into his calculator, divided it by 27 then read off the twelve digits to the left of the decimal point. He entered them into the terminal and hit RETURN. The screen came to life with Thurgood-Smythe's nodding image.

'Very glad to see that you have arrived safely, Jan, and are now with my old associate Amri Ben-Haim. As you must realize this recording is far too important to have risked accidental disclosure. Ben-Haim had half the key to it, you Jan the other as you have now discovered. Now please make yourself comfortable while I explain what I have in mind.'

Jan touched the STOP button and Thurgood-Smythe's image froze on the screen. 'Don't you think we ought to record this?' he asked. 'This disc is liable to self-destruct for all we know, so a copy is very much in order.'

'Of course,' Ben-Haim said. 'Please do that.'

Jan slipped a blank disc into one of the drives then started the recording again.

'. . . I want the present war of rebellion to end as soon as possible. Ben-Haim, Jan will tell you my personal reasons behind this decision. I suppose you will not believe them any more than he does, which is a pity. I am most sincere in this matter. But that is beside the point. The arrangements I suggest to end the war will appeal to you on completely pragmatic grounds. I count upon self-interest to secure your aid, not sympathy for any cause I might espouse.

'Firstly I shall outline the grand design of my plan so you will understand it and realize that circumstance will force you to join me in implementing it. I'm sure that we share a mutual goal in believing that the coming conflict must end with victory for the human race.

'Details. My intelligence sources reveal that a large force of ships is on the way towards Earth. This has been hastily assembled and is made up of every deep spaceship in serviceable condition. The planets are gambling their future, their very existence on this single try. Of course they have no other choice. Earth policy has always been to keep the manufacturing of all industrial and space drive components safely here on Earth. As key control equipment breaks down it will not be replaced. The same applies to the fuel and basic circuitry for the Foscolo space drive. Now that all of the Earth forces have withdrawn the only thing the rebel forces can do is attack. It must be done sooner or later – and soonest is best before the attrition of time begins to takes it toll of the machinery. I do not know the details of the rebels plans, but I do know that there is one thing that they must do if they hope to win. They must attack and capture the Mojave base of Spaceconcent. Any other course would be suicidal. All supplies essential for the existence of the space forces go through here. If it is captured or destroyed that is the end of the defensive forces.

'This will be accomplished in the following manner. Firstly attacks must be made in space to divide the strength of the defending fleet. Then the Mojave complex must be captured. This will have to be done from the ground since the missile defences are too strong to penetrate from space. After capture the victory will be secured by the landing of the attackers. Surrender and final victory will follow.

'Now for details. Jan, I will arrange for you to contact the rebel fleet in order to coordinate the operation. When this is done the Israeli forces will attack and capture Spaceconcent, and will hold it until relieved. Before they make a decision on whether to take part, I wish to remind them of the raid on Entebbe and the rising in the Warsaw ghetto. It is time to leave the ghetto again . . . '

Jan stopped the replay and turned to Ben-Haim. 'I think the man's mad. What were those last things he was talking about?'

'Not mad – but criminally sane. He tempts us with salvation knowing that it could mean destruction. And in order to help us decide, he quotes from our own history. His thinking is as convoluted as that of a Talmudic scholar.'

'The Warsaw rising was during the Second World War,' Dvora said. 'Jews were being slaughtered there by the Nazis, were dying of starvation and disease as well. They rose up and fought their attackers, bare hands against guns, until they were all killed. They knew they would die – but they would not submit.'

'And equally important,' Ben-Haim added, 'they fought to break out of the ghetto. And still, today, the Jews are forced to live in a ghetto. It may be an entire country but, comfortable as it is – it is still a ghetto. Thurgood-Smythe knows that we want to leave.'

'And Entebbe?' Jan asked. 'What was that?'

'A commando raid half way around the world that should not have stood a chance of succeeding. But it did.

Thurgood-Smythe puts Satan to shame with his temptations!'

'I don't quite understand these temptations,' Jan said. 'You're not threatened or at war with anyone. You can just sit this one out and see what happens.'

'Basically, that is quite true. But in a very real sense our freedom is but an illusion of freedom. We are free to stay in our nation-wide jail. There is also an ironical sense of justice and injustice that appeals to us. We in our little free prison are surrounded by a world of economic and physically enslaved *goyem*. Shouldn't we help them? We who were in bondage for millennia know well what it is. Should we not aid others to achieve what we always prayed for for ourselves? I said, this is a riddle for Talmudic scholars. I'm old so perhaps I doubt too much. I like my security. But here is the voice of young Israel. Dvora – what do you think?'

'I don't think – I know!' she said fiercely. 'Fight! There is no other course possible.'

'My response is equally simple,' Jan said. 'If there is any chance at all of this thing succeeding I must go along with it. Thurgood-Smythe says that he will put me in contact with the attacking fleet. Very good for not only will I tell them about his plan, but I can tell them also about our reservations and what kind of twister Thurgood-Smythe really is. Then the responsibility for a final decision will not rest with me. So my response is clearcut. I do what he says.'

'Yes, in your position I would do the same,' Ben-Haim said. 'You have nothing to lose – but the world to gain. Yet it all sounds too good. I have the feeling that the man must be playing a devious game.'

'That doesn't matter,' Dvora said. 'His personal fate should not concern us. If this is all a trap then the attackers must be warned and turn the knowledge to their advantage. If it is not a trap Israel must fight in this final battle, this war to end all wars.'

Ben-Haim sighed deeply and rocked back and forth in his chair. 'How many times have those words been spoken? The war to end all wars. Have they ever been true?'

'No. But they could be now,' Dvora insisted. 'Turn it on again, Jan. Let's hear the end of it.'

It made a lot of sense – or nonsense. Jan felt himself as entrapped as the Israelis. Basically the one thing he wanted to do with Thurgood-Smythe was kill him. Instead he found himself working for him. He shook his head in wonderment and reached out and touched the button.

' . . . time to leave the ghetto again. So think carefully about what I have said. Weigh your decisions. Take the Knesset into your confidence and ask then for a decision. There are no separate parts to this proposal. You must accept it or reject it. It's all or nothing. This is the only argument from me that you will hear. There is time, but not very much, to reach your decision. The attacking fleet will be here in approximately ten days. Your attack will take place just before dawn on the date that you will be given. You have four days to decide. On next Friday night your radio station will be broadcasting the usual weekly memorial service to honour those who have passed on. If you wish to take part simply list Jan Kulozik's name among the noble dead. He is not a superstitous man so I am sure he will not mind. However, if you decide not to participate in the salvation of mankind simply do nothing – since you will be doing nothing. You will not hear from me again.'

'Such guilt he gives us,' Ben-Haim said as the screen went dark. 'Are you sure he was never trained in theology?'

'I am sure of nothing about my brother-in-law. Though

I am sure now that all of his earlier background is his own invention. Perhaps he is the father of lies, just as you said. What will you do next?'

'Just as he commanded. Take the proposal to the Knesset, our parliament. Let a little of the responsibility and guilt slip off onto their shoulders.'

Dvora and Jan left the room when Ben-Haim turned to the telephone. They had not noticed, because of the automatic lighting, that darkness had fallen while they had been listening to Thurgood-Smythe. They went out onto the balcony, not speaking, each of them wrapped in private thought. Jan leaned against a pillar and looked out at the ascending lights of the town, where it climbed up the side of the darkened valley across from him. It was a moonless night and the stars burned clear and sharp, filling the sky as far down as the black cut-out of the horizon. A world at peace, comfortable and secure. And Thurgood-Smythe wanted them to give it all up, to go to war for an ideal. Jan did not envy them their decision; his had been easy enough to make. Turning around he saw that Dvora was sitting on the couch, quietly, her hands folded in her lap.

'You must be hungry,' she said. 'Let me fix you something.'

'In a moment. What do you think the Knesset will do?'

'Talk. They are very good at that. Just a bunch of old men who prefer talk to action. Thurgood-Smythe should have given them four months to make their minds up instead of four days?'

'Then you don't think they will decide?'

'They'll decide all right. Against the idea. Play it safe, they always want to play it safe.'

'Perhaps that's how they got to be old men.'

'Are you laughing at me? Let me see your face.'

Dvora pulled him down next to her on the couch and saw that indeed he was smiling. She could not help smiling back.

'All right, so I am getting angry over nothing. It hasn't happened yet. But it will, just as I said it would. Then I'll get angry. But if that happens what will you do? In case they say no.'

'I haven't begun to even think about that possibility. Go back and get in touch with Thurgood-Smythe again I imagine. I just can't stay safely here when the fate of everyone in the world – all of the worlds – is being decided. Perhaps I can still contact the attacking fleet, tell them what I know. There's no point in trying to decide before I have to.'

While he was talking Jan realized that they still had their hands clasped together; neither would pull away from the bond. What am I thinking of, Jan worried, then became aware that he wasn't thinking at all. But feeling, reacting physically. And he knew, without asking, that Dvora felt the same way. He wanted to question the sensation but did not, was afraid to. When he turned towards her she was already facing him. Then, without conscious effort, she was in his arms.

An unmeasurable space of time passed before she drew her mouth away from his, but still held him tightly in her arms. Her words were only a whisper.

'Come to my room. This place is far too public.'

He stood up when she did but tried hard to express the tiny niggle of doubt that tapped at him.

'I'm married, Dvora. My wife, light years away . . . '

She touched her finger to his lips.

'Shh. It's chemistry not matrimony I have in mind. Just follow me.'

He did. Quite willingly.

# Chapter Thirteen

'We never did get anything to eat,' Jan said.

'You are a very greedy person,' Dvora answered. 'For most men this would be enough.'

She kicked the covering sheet from her and stretched the brown length of her naked body in the morning sunlight that streamed through the window. Jan ran his fingertips down her side and across the tight rise of her stomach. She shivered at his touch.

'I'm so glad that I'm alive,' she said. 'Being dead must be very grey and boring. This is so much more fun.'

Jan smiled and reached for her, but she pulled away and stood up, a splendid, warm-fleshed sculpture as she arched her back and ran her fingers through her hair. Then reached for a dressing gown.

'You're the one who mentioned food, not me,' she said. 'But now that you have raised the subject I realize that I'm starving. Come along and I'll fix us some breakfast.'

'I better get to my own room first.'

She laughed at this, pulling the comb through her knotted hair. 'Why? We're not children here. We're adults. We come and go as we please, do as we please. What sort of a world do you come from?'

'Not that kind. Not now at least. Though in London – God, it seems like centuries ago – I suppose I was very much my own person. Until I got in the way of the authorities. Since then I have been living in a social nightmare. I can't begin to tell you the ugliness and restrictions of life on Halvmörk – nor do I intend to try. Breakfast is a far better idea.'

The plumbing was functional, instead of ultra-luxurious like the Waldorf-Astoria. He approved of it this way he realized, as the pipes gurgled and clanked and finally produced hot water. It worked – and he was sure that everyone in the country had one that was just as good. A concept of democracy he had not considered before. Equality of physical comfort as well as equality of opportunity. A growl of hunger in his midriff drove all philosophical thoughts away; he quickly washed and dressed. Then followed his nose to a large, open kitchen, where a young man and a woman sat at a long trestle table. They nodded as he came in and Dvora handed him a steaming mug of coffee.

'Food first, introductions later,' she said. 'How do you like your eggs?'

'On a plate.'

'Intelligent decision. There's some *matzoh brei* here which will introduce you to good heavy kosher cooking if you have not had that pleasure before.'

The young couple waved and slipped away without being introduced. Jan realized then that few names would be exchanged here in the heart of the secret service. Dvora served them both at the same time and sat down across from him. She ate with as good an appetite as he did, while they chatted lightly about totally unimportant things. They were just finishing up when the other girl returned, bursting into the room. Her smile was gone now.

'Ben-Haim wants you both right away. It's trouble, big trouble.'

The atmosphere was thick with it. Ben-Haim sat slumped wearily in the same chair where they had left him the night before, where he might very well have been the entire time. He was sucking on a pipe long dead and seemed completely unaware of it.

'It appears that Thurgood-Smythe is putting on some

111

pressure. I should have realized that he would not simply ask for a favour from us. That's not his way.'

'What happened?' Dvora asked.

'Raids. Right around the world in every country. Reports are still coming in. Protective custody, they say. Because of the emergency. Our people, all of them. Business representatives and trade missions, even secret operatives we thought were still secret. He's got them, all of them, arrested. Two thousand, maybe more.'

'Pressure,' Jan said. 'He's tightening the screw. Have you considered what else he might do?'

'What else can he do? The few thousand of our citizens that he has taken into custody are the only ones who, legally or illegally, are outside Israel and the adjoining countries. He has them all.'

'I'm sure that he is up to something. I know Thurgood-Smythe's manner of operation by now, and this is just the first step.'

Jan was unhappily proved right within the hour. All of the television programs, on every one of the hundred and twelve channels, were interrupted with news of an important announcement. It would be carried on every channel and would be presented by Doctor Bal Ram Mahant, the President of the United Nations. The position was an honorary one, and the Doctor's activities were usually confined to opening and closing UN sessions. However he did make the occasional important announcement such as this one. A military brass band played patriotic marches while the world watched – and waited. The band's image faded and Doctor Mahant appeared. He nodded his head at the unseen audience and began to speak in his familiar, high-pitched voice.

'Citizens of the world. We are in the midst of a terrible war brought to us by anarchist elements among the body of faithful citizens of the planets of the great Commonwealth of Earth. But I am not here to discuss that now, that great battle that our citizen-soldiers are waging and winning for the freedom of mankind. I am here to tell you of an even greater threat to our security. Certain individuals in the United Nations Conclave of Israel have been holding back vital food supplies for their own benefit. They are war profiteers, making money out of the starvation of others. This will not be permitted to continue. They must be made to understand the error of their ways. Justice must be done before others try to follow their example.'

Doctor Mahant sighed; the weight of responsibility for the world was upon his shoulders. But he accepted the burden and went on.

'Even as I talk our soldiers are moving into Egypt, Jordan, Syria and all of the other important food producing countries in this area. No one of you will go hungry, that I promise you. Food shipments will continue despite the efforts of the selfish minority. Rebellion will be put down and we will march on together to victory.'

The President faded from view to the accompaniment of jubilant recorded applause and his image was replaced by the blue and white flag of Earth cracking in the wind. The brass band played enthusiastically. Ben-Haim turned off the set.

'I don't understand,' Jan said.

'I do, only too well,' Ben-Haim answered. 'You are forgetting that the rest of the world does not even know that our nation exists. They will be only too happy to see these countries occupied to make sure their bellies stay full. These are lands of peasant farmers for the most part, shipping out their produce through their cooperatives. But we are the ones who taught them how to irrigate and fertilize the desert to grow these crops, and we are the ones who set up their marketing boards as well. And our country has handled all of the external shipments with our fleet of air transports. Until now. Now do you see what he is doing to us? We are being pushed out, sent back within our own borders. And more attrition will follow. This is all Thurgood-Smythe's doing. No one else cares about the fate of this tiny corner of the world, not at this time. And see what a good student of history he is. With what care he revives those sneering twentieth century terms of approbation, those anti-semitic labels that surely date back to medieval Europe. Profiteers, usurers, getting rich while others starve. His message is very clear.'

Jan nodded. 'Forcing your hand. If you don't do as he ordered the country is going to suffer.'

'Either way we suffer. We lose – or we lose. As long as the big powers of the world paid no attention to us we survived. Our tiny balance of terror, our few atom bombs in exchange for their myriad atom bombs made us not worth bothering about. As long as we kept peace in the Near East, stayed humbly in this area – and saw that they had continuous supplies of fresh oranges and avocados in the winter time, why then we just weren't worth bothering about. Now Thurgood-Smythe is tightening the clamps and this war gives him a perfect excuse. Their troops will move in slowly, up to our borders. We can't stop them. They'll occupy all of our external missile sites. When that is done they can drop their bombs or send in the tanks. It makes no difference. We lose either way.'

'And Thurgood-Smythe will do it,' Jan said angrily. 'Not out of revenge for your not helping him – that would be a show of emotion, and an emotional person can always be appealed to, possibly convinced to change his mind. But Thurgood-Smythe will proceed calmly to do this, even if all of his plans fail. What he begins he finishes. He wants you to be sure of that.'

'You know him very well,' Ben-Haim said, looking

closely at Jan. 'Wheels within wheels. I can see why he sent you as emissary. There was really no need to have you carry his message in person. But he wanted us to be absolutely sure of his resolve, to know exactly what kind of a man he really was. So you are the devil's advocate, God help you, whether you like it or not. We are back once again to the father of lies. Best not to let the rabbis get hold of this theory or they will have us all believing it.'

'What are we to do?' Dvora asked, her voice empty and lost.

'The Knesset must be convinced that our only chance now is to procede along the lines Thurgood-Smythe has laid out. I will have the radio message sent that we will cooperate, whether the Knesset has agreed or not by that time. They'll come around in the end. They have no alternative. And then there will have to be a second diaspora.'

'Why? What do you mean?'

'The diaspora occurred when the Jews were expelled from the land of Israel, thousands of years ago. This time we will go voluntarily. If the attack on the Mojave base fails their retribrution will be instant – and atomic. This entire tiny country will become a radioactive pit. We must therefore plan to reduce the mortality if we can. There will have to be volunteers who will stay behind to keep the services going and conceal our withdrawal. Everyone else will leave, quietly, by filtering out into the surrounding countries where we have our good Arab friends. Hopefully, if the raid is a successful one, they will be able to come home again. If not, well, we have carried our religion and our culture with us before to alien lands. We will survive.'

Dvora nodded in grim agreement and Jan knew for the first time what had kept these people going through the millennia, despite the worst kind of persecution. He knew that they would be in the future as they were in the past.

Ben-Haim shook himself, like someone upon whom a chilling wind has blown. He took the cold pipe from his mouth and stared at it as though he had just become aware of its presence. Laying it carefully on the table he rose and went slowly from the room, walking like an old man for the first time. Dvora watched him go, then turned to Jan and held him tightly, her face pressed against his chest, as though finding some security there to ward off the dark future hurrying towards them.

'I wonder where it will end,' she said, in a voice so quiet he could barely hear it.

'In peace for all mankind. You're the one who said it. The war to end all wars. I have been in this fight from the beginning. Now, like it or not, it looks like your people are as well. I just wish I knew what Thurgood-Smythe was thinking. Whether this is a plot to destroy us – or to bring lasting peace. I just wish that I knew.'

It was late in the afternoon, almost dusk, when the helicopter arrived, dropping out of the sky with a roar of engines and blades. Jan and Dvora were in the garden when he was sent for.

'Look at this,' Ben-Haim said, pointing to the sealed suitcase on the floor. 'Special delivery for you from the United Nations in Tel-Aviv. They brought it to our supposedly secret office next door to them, the one that monitors their communications. The manner of delivery identifies its sender. It is a message for me that they know more about our operations than we think they do. And for you – you will have to look and see,'

'Hasn't it been opened?'

'Sealed shut. With a combination lock. Dare we guess that we know the correct number by now? And no need to send Dvora to the bottom of the garden to open this one.

Our friend has bigger goals than blowing up an old man. May I?'

Without waiting for an answer Ben-Haim leaned forward and touched the buttons in quick succession. The lock clicked as it unsealed itself. Jan picked up the case and put it on the table, opened it.

There was a black uniform inside, black boots and a matching cloth cap with a starburst insignia on it. Lying on top of the clothing was a transparent plastic envelope. It contained an ID card in the name of John Halliday and a thick technical manual with a computer disc inside the cover. Tucked into the manual so it projected a bit was a brief note. It was addressed to Jan. He took it up and read it aloud.

'John Halliday is a UNO technician working at the communications centre in Cairo. He is also in the Space Forces Reserve where he is a communications technician. You will master this occupation very quickly, Jan, and the enclosed manual should help. You have two full days to learn the job and to get to Cairo. Your friends in Israel will be able to arrange that without your being detected en route. Once in the city I suggest you wear this uniform and go directly to the airport. Your orders will be waiting at the Security desk there. I wish you good luck. We are all depending on you.' Jan looked up. 'That's all it says. It's unsigned.'

It did not have to be. They all knew that Thurgood-Smythe's plans had moved forward one more notch.

# Chapter Fourteen

'You cut it pretty fine, soldier,' the Security man said, looking Jan up and down coldly as though trying to find an open button in his uniform. There was none.

'I got here as soon as I heard,' Jan said,

'Just because you're over here enjoying the luxuries of life don't mean you're exempt from your duties.'

As he proceeded with the ritual chastisement, the Security officer slipped the ID into his terminal and nodded to Jan, who placed the fingertips of his right hand on the identification plate. Almost as exact as a retinal print and much faster to use for normal identification. The ID was ejected and handed back to Jan, his identity accepted. Thurgood-Smythe must have access to identification files at the topmost level – with no one to monitor his actions.

'Well, sir, it looks like they're giving you first class transportation.' The change in the Security man's attitude was very abrupt and Jan knew that his new status was far higher than the man had expected. 'There's a military jet on the way for you now. If you would like to wait in the bar I'll have someone come and get you when the plane arrives. Is that all right? I'll look after your bag for you.'

Jan nodded and headed for the bar, not as pleased with his new high-ranking status as Security was. He was by himself, completely alone. It is one thing to consider that in theory, another to actually be subjected to it. The shadowy form of Thurgood-Smythe lurked behind him all of the time, but that just made him more insecure. A pawn on a chessboard with Thurgood-Smythe manipulating all of the pieces. Not for the first time did he wonder just what the man was planning.

The beer was tasteless but cold and he limited himself to one bottle. This was not a day to have a thick head. He was alone with the Egyptian bartender who solemnly polished glass after glass in silence. There was apparently little traffic through Cairo airport. Nor was there any sign of the occupation troops that featured so largely in President Mahant's speech. Had it all been a ruse? There was no way of telling. But his position was real enough and he was not looking forward to the coming encounters with any great enthusiasm. Events were rushing past him, getting ahead of him so that it was growing more and more difficult to keep up with the accelerating changes. The boring years he had spent on Halvmörk seemed almost attractive by comparison. When he returned – if he returned – life would be quiet and satisfactory. He would have a family there, his wife, a child on the way, more children. The future of the planet to worry about. Alzbeta; she had scarcely been in his thoughts at all of late. Too little time. He saw her now in his mind's eye, smiling, her arms out to him. But it was hard to hold this image; it melted away, was overlaid with the far stronger one of Dvora, naked and close, the musky smell of her body in his nostrils . . .

Damn! He drained his glass and signalled for a second one. Life was very complex. As dangerous as it had been since his arrival back on Earth it also had been . . . what? Fun? No, he couldn't call it that. Interesting, it was surely that, and damn exciting once he knew that he was going to live for at least a little bit longer. He shouldn't be thinking about the future now, not until he was sure that he was going to have one. Wait and see, that was all that he could do.

'Technician Halliday,' the PA system said. 'Technician Halliday to Gate Three.'

Jan heard the message twice before it penetrated that it was for him. His new identity. He put down his glass and headed for Gate Three. The same Security officer was waiting for him there.

'If you'll come with me, sir. The plane's been refuelled and is ready to go. Your bag's aboard already.'

Jan nodded and followed the man out into the heat of the day, the sun reflected and glaring from the white concrete. They came to a supersonic two-place fighter marked with the white star of the United States Air Force; travel in style indeed. The mechanics held the stairs as Jan climbed aboard, one of them following him up to close and seal the hatch. The pilot turned and waved his hand over his shoulder in greeting.

'Someone sure in a hurry to get your ass out of here. Pulled me out of a poker game, never even let me play my hand. Strap in.'

The jets roared and vibrated beneath them and they were airborne almost as soon as they turned into the runway.

'Where are we going,' Jan asked, as soon as the gear was up and they were in a steady climb up to cruising altitude. 'Mojave?'

'Shit no. I wish we were. I've been out in a desert field here so long I'm beginning to grow a hump like a camel. And hump, real hump, that's what I'd be getting if I were flying into Mojave. No we're vectored right into Baikonur, soon as I get above the commercial lanes. Them Russkies don't like no one, even themselves. Lock you in a little room, guards with guns everywhere. Sign eight thousand goddamn forms for the fuel. Get crabs from the furniture, I swear I know an old boy lay over there and got

120

crabs. Says they jump further then Texas crabs and they jump fourteen feet . . . '

It took no large effort to tune out the pilot's reminiscences. Apparently his voice worked separately from his mind because he flew the plane with great precision, instrument and navigation checks and all. Without shutting up for a second.

Baikonur. Somewhere in southern Russia, that's all Jan remembered. Not an important base, too small for anything other than orbital lifters. Probably just there to prove that the Soviets were members of the big nation club. He was undoubtedly going to be put into space from there. With no idea yet of his final destination.

Wartime had intensified the traditional Russian paranoia and the tower at Baikonur was in continual radio contact with the pilot as soon as they had started across the Black Sea.

'This is a security warning, Air Force four three niner, and must be obeyed exactly. Any deviation will cause automatic reprisal. Do you read me?'

'Read you? For Christ's sake, Baikonur, I told you I did, about seventeen god damned times now! My autopilot's locked on your frequency, I am steady at your specified height of twenty thousand. I'm just a passenger in this plane so you bring it in and talk to your machinery if you want to issue any more orders.'

Unmoved, the deep voice carried on insistantly.

'No deviation will be allowed. Do you read me Air Force four three niner?'

'I read you, I read you,' the pilot said wearily. Defeated by Slavic stolidity.

It was night when they crossed the Soviet shore and began their approach to the space complex. The lights of towns and cities swept by beneath them, but Baikonur itself was completely blacked out because of the hostilities. It was disconcerting to see that the plane was dropping lower and lower towards the ground while still completely under airport control. It is one thing to know abstractly that radar and electronic communications need no light, that they work just as well in complete darkness; still another to hear the wing flaps grinding into position, the landing gear locking down – when there is nothing visible in any direction. All of this was controlled by the computer on the ground – the ground which was still totally invisible in the darkness ahead. The aircraft's landing lights stayed off, as did the runway lights. Jan found that he was holding his breath as the engine throttled back and they dropped. To make a perfect landing on the still invisible runway. Only when they had come to a complete stop at the end of the taxiway was control returned to the pilot.

'Feel like a goddamned passenger,' he muttered to himself, settling his infra-red goggles firmly into place. The FOLLOW ME car finally arrived and they taxied after it into a blacked out hangar; the lights came on only after the door was closed. Jan blinked in the sudden glare as he unbuckled his straps. An officer, wearing the same black uniform as his, was waiting at the foot of the steps.

'Technician Halliday?'

'Yes, sir.'

'Get your bag and come with me. There's a supply shuttle on line now with a window coming up in about twenty minutes. We can make it if we hurry. Let's go.'

After this, Jan was just a passenger. The chemical fuelled rocket boosted into a low orbit that was barely outside the atmosphere. A deep space fusion shuttle locked to them and the passengers, all military personnel, transferred to this. Every one of them was at home in null-G. Jan was thankful that he had worked in space

122

before or his clumsiness would have given him away instantly. Once in their seats they had to wait while the cargo was transferred as well; in the interval they enjoyed the dubious pleasure of a Russian squeezepak meal. It had a soapy texture and tasted vaguely of fish. Afterwards Jan read the instructions on the free fall toilet very carefully before he used it. There were as many disaster stories about its use as there were about the equivalent bit of sanitary engineering that was fitted into submarines.

Boredom very quickly replaced tension, since there was little to do other than look at recordings or catch up on sleep. The space colony of Lagrange 5 was unluckily almost at its maximum distance from Earth, nearly 200,000 miles, so the trip was a long one. While pretending to doze, Jan eavesdropped shamelessly on his fellow spacemen. The colony was being used as a base for the Space Force and headquarters for the Earth defence fleet, he discovered. Most of the conversation seemed to be a mixture of rumour and gossip and he memorized the best bits to be used as part of his cover.

He quickly discovered when talking with the others that most of them were reservists who had never served in the regular Space Force before. This was encouraging, since it would help to cover any ommisions or slips on his part. As it turned out these precautions were not necessary; Thurgood-Smythe had planned his future quite precisely. When they finally docked and disembarked at Lagrange 5, Jan never even had the opportunity to see the interior of the manufacturing colony. A messenger was waiting in the spacelock chamber as they emerged.

'Technician Halliday,' he shouted as the men floated by him. 'Which one of you is Tech Halliday?'

Jan hesitated just an instant before he kicked off in the

123

man's direction. His cover could not have been discovered; this development had to be part of Thurgood-Smythe's complex planning. It was.

'Get suited up and leave your gear here, Halliday. It'll be waiting when you get back. We got a scout going out and we're one tech short. You're the lucky lad who's elected.' He looked at the printout he held. 'Commander name of Captain Lastrup. Ship's the Ida Peter Two Five Six. Let's go.'

They used a jaxter, an open skeletal framework with six metal seats fixed to it. Other than this it was little more than four jets and a control pedestal. The pilot was familiar with the little craft and kicked it away from the airlock, flipped it end for end neatly, and was on a new trajectory even before their turn was complete.

The fleet of Earth made an impressive sight. Grouped around the two kilometre long colony were scores of deep space vessels of all sizes. They ranged from gigantic bulk carriers down to jaxters like the one they were in, with a spectrum of sizes, shapes and functions in between. Their course took them in an arc up over the fleet towards the shining needle of a scoutship. The crew quarters in the bow were tiny in comparison to the engines and auxiliary fuel tanks to the rear. It bristled with antennae and detection devices of all kinds. In space, beyond the fixed network of early warning stations, it was ships like this that were the eyes and ears of the fleet. The jaxter floated towards it, slowed and stopped with a quick flare of the bow jet. The large characters of identification were painted across the bow, IP-256, just above the open door of the spacelock. Jan unbuckled his safety belt, floated free of the seat, then pushed off towards the ship. He drifted gently into the lock, seized one of the grabirons, and waved back to the jaxter pilot as he pressed the cycle button. The outer port ground slowly shut.

When the pressure in the airlock equalled that in the ship the inner lock opened automatically. Jan cracked his helmet and floated inside. The circular chamber, obviously the living quarters, couldn't have been more than three metres across and just about as high. Around nine cubic metres of living space for two men, Jan estimated. Wonderful. No expenses spared to make our boys in space comfortable.

A man's head appeared through a circular opening in the bow end of the room, upside down to Jan's orientation. A red face with slightly bulging eyes.

'Not accomplishing very much, are you, Tech, just floating around and sightseeing.' This undoubtedly was Captain Lastrup. A fine spray of saliva exploded in Jan's direction with every angry word. 'Just peel out of that suit and get up here on the double.'

'Yes, sir,' Jan said, obeying instructions.

Within two hours, after they had unlocked from their moorings and got under way, Jan was beginning to dislike the Captain. By the time he was permitted to retire, more than twenty hours after his arrival, he loathed the man. It was painful, after only three hours sleep, to be dragged back to blurry consciousness and summoned to the control room.

'I'm going to close my eyes for a bit, Tech Halliday, which means that you are on watch. Don't touch anything or do anything because you are just a totally incompetent reservist amateur. The machines will do all the things you are incapable of doing. If there is a little red warning light or a little beeping warning sound you are to awaken me at once. Understood?'

'Yes, sir. But I am capable of monitoring the equipment because I know ... '

'Did I ask for your opinion? Did I order you to talk? Anything you have to say is just shit to me, mister.

Understood? If you answer anything more than yessir that will be disobeying orders and that will go into the charges against you. Now, what do you say?'

Jan was tired, getting angrier with every passing moment. He said nothing and he enjoyed the red glow that suffused the officer's skin with every passing silent second.

'I order you to speak!'

Jan slowly counted to five before he said 'Yes, sir.'

It was very small revenge for the verbal abuse he was taking. But it was enough for the moment. Jan took an Awake pill and tried not to rub at his sore and grainy eyes. Only the softest red glow illuminated the control room. Stars filled the viewport ahead; flickering readouts and displays from the detection apparatus monitored space in all directions. They were passing through the outer web now and very soon their reports would be the only early warning in this particular portion of space. Although he had received no instructions from Thurgood-Smythe, Jan knew exactly what to do in this situation.

They were heading away from Earth, at full acceleration, into space, in the direction of the attacking fleet. The orbiting radio telescopes had detected objects out here, at maximum range, in a portion of space where nothing should be. The IP-256 was on its way to scout what could only be the rebel space fleet. Jan would control his anger and do nothing to irritate Captain Lastrup any further. He regretted losing his temper and speaking out of turn, then aggravating the offence by adding dumb insolence to it as well. As soon as the Captain came on duty he would apologize to him. After that Jan would do his best to be a good spaceman and would work as hard as he could to do exactly as he was told. He would do this with all the effort of will that he could muster. He would keep doing this until they had pinpointed the attackers and

126

were absolutely certain of their identification and position.

At that time Jan was going to use a one metre length of thick electrical wire. He had it cut and ready, and would then experience the sweet and satisfying pleasure of strangling the military son of a bitch.

# *Chapter Fifteen*

'Got them, look at the size of that fleet – is this going into memory, Tech? If it's not I'll ... '

'Going in fine, sir,' Jan said. 'Onto disc storage with a backup on molecular wafer. I've replayed both and they're perfect.'

'They better be, they had better be,' Captain Lastrup muttered savagely. 'I'm setting up a return course now. As soon as the main dish bears on Earth squirt out the readings with maximum watts. Got that?'

'Absolutely, sir. This is the moment I have been waiting for.'

There was true joy in Jan's voice. As he spoke he was carefully wrapping the ends of the thick wire around and around each of his hands. He snapped it tight and looked at it thoughtfully. About seventy centimetres in length; that should do nicely. Without releasing his grip on the wire he unclipped from his seat and kicked off towards the pilot, twisting neatly in midflight to approach head first with his arms extended before him.

Lastrup had a glimpse of the moving figure out of the corner of his eye. He turned and had just enough time for a look of shocked amazement before the stretched wire dropped beneath his chin and was locked into place by the swift crossing of Jan's arms.

Jan had given careful thought to this operation for a long time, planned every part of it precisely. A steady tightening now of the wire, not a sharp snap that might crush the man's throat. He did not want to kill him, just secure him. It was a silent struggle, punctuated only by

Jan's heavy breathing. The Captain was of course not breathing at all. He struggled a bit but could do nothing. His eyes closed and his body went limp very quickly. Jan loosened the wire, ready to tighten it instantly if the man was shamming. He wasn't; he was deeply unconscious, breathing hoarsely but regularly, with a strong pulse in his neck. Perfect. Jan used the wire to lash the officer's hands securely behind his back, and then tied another length about his ankles. There was more than enough trailing wire from his wrists to secure the unconscious officer to the rear bulkhead out of harm's way.

First step done. Jan did not bother to waste a glance at the ship's controls. He had examined them closely during his time on watch alone and had very quickly determined that he was not going to become a deep space pilot by calling up the instruction manuals from memory. They took for granted too much previous knowledge. Therefore he had relied on the simple and archaic statement by Newton that any object in motion tends to remain in motion, in a straight line and at a constant velocity. That object now was the IP-256 and the straight line was pointed rather accurately at the approaching rebel ships. It was the pilot's decision to alter that course that had produced his abrupt lapse into unconsciousness. The course change he wanted had been computed and was ready for implementation. Which was the last thing that Jan had in mind. With the pilot secured and forgotten, he turned to his equipment panels.

It was too much to expect that their two courses would coincide and that this ship would meet the attackers head on. This did not matter at all if Jan could establish contact with them. He switched on the power and swung the largest dish antenna so it pointed at the fleet. Exact allignment would not be necessary; even the tightest signal he could broadcast would be far greater in diameter than the fleet by the time it reached them. He cranked the power to maximum, hooked a recorder into the line, then swung the bead microphone into position before his mouth.

'This is Jan Kulozik calling, from Earth scout ship IP-256 now closing upon your present position. This signal is highly directional and beamed at you. Don't, repeat don't, make any attempt to answer at this time. Please record this message. Message follows.

'I was resident on Halvmörk and left that planet with a food ship comanded by a man named Debhu. We were captured in orbit by Earth forces and made prisoner. Later all the prisoners were killed; I'm the only survivor. I will give you all the details later but tell you this now so you will understand who I am. Please do not fire on this ship when we get within range. This is a two-man scout and I have secured the commander. I do not know how to pilot this vessel nor do I intend to learn at the present time. The ship is not armed. Here is what I suggest you do.

'As soon as you have computed my course and velocity dispatch one of your spacers on a closing course to match my speed. I will do nothing to alter any vectors, but I will open the airlock. I am familiar with spacesuit operations and will transfer to your ship. I suggest sending a pilot to take over this scout since it contains highly sophisticated detection gear.

'You have no reason to believe me, but also have no reason not to capture this scout. I also have information of highest priority about Earth defences and coming operations there.

'I am broadcasting now on the emergency frequency. I am recording and this message will automatically repeat on the two main communication frequencies, then the emergency frequency again. It will be continous until we meet. Message ends.'

After this Jan could only wait. And begin to worry. He kept his receivers on and picked up a number of coded messages from Earth fleet command directed at the IP-256, all of which he cheerfully ignored. It would be best if the enemy forces thought that the scoutship had vanished completely. This could only cause dismay, and hopefully a good bit of confusion, perhaps even make them think about possible secret weapons that the rebels might possess. Yet Jan was still worried. His plan was a good one, the only possible one, but it required a great deal of patience. Since he had received no communications from the attacking fleet it could mean that his message had been received and that the instructions were being carried out. Or that everything had gone wrong and they were heading swiftly into interstellar space. Or even worse, that there had been a mistaken identification of the ships approaching Earth, that they were defending not attacking forces. Once he had started to worry, he found a great deal to worry about.

Captain Lastrup did not make life any easier. As soon as he had regained consciousness he began a continuous and high-pitched description of what would happen to Jan after he had been returned to justice. Saliva ran down his chin, unnoticed by him in the intensity of his feelings, while his voice grew hoarse and rasping. Jan tried to stem the flow by threatening to get the throttling wire out again, but this had no effect. Then he warned that he would gag the captain, and when this made not the slightest difference he actually put the threat into practice. But the sight of the bulging eyes, the face gradually turning from red to purple as Lastrup swung and writhed and bounced off the bulkhead was too much, too inhumane. He ungagged the man and turned the radio on loud to roar counterpoint to the ravings.

Two days went by like this, with the Captain dozing off

for blessed minutes in his bindings, only to awake and resume the tirade again. He would not eat, spat out the food that Jan tried to feed him, but did drink some water. Undoubtedly to keep his voice in good operating order. When Jan let him use the sanitary facilities he fought to escape and in the end Jan had to wire him to the apparatus. It was very uncomfortable for both of them. Therefore it was a tremendous relief for Jan on the third day when he found a weak blip at the outermost edge of the low power radar screen he was broadcasting. It was approaching on what very well might be a converging course. He killed the recorded broadcast, dropped the power down to the weakest signal possible. And crossed his fingers.

'This is Kulozik on IP-256. I have a blip on my radar. Do you read me?'

The radio frequency rustle of the stars was all he heard. He sent the signal again, stepped up the gain on his receiver – then heard it, weakly but there.

'Do not alter course, IP-256. Do not attempt to start your engines for any reason. Do not attempt any more broadcasts. If you do we will fire. Open your outer port but do not attempt to leave your ship or we will fire. Out.'

Definitely warlike, Jan thought. But he would probably be doing the same thing if he were in their place. He killed his radar and radio transmitter, but left the receiver on since it was well shielded and produced no detectable emissions. After that all he could do was evacuate the airlock and open the outer hatch. And wait.

'My friends are coming,' he said, with more assurance than he really felt. This had not the slightest effect on his captive who described Jan's tortured future for the thousandth time. It was not pleasurable to hear and having the Captain removed from his earshot would be one of the major pleasures that would come with the end of this trip.

Something clattered in the airlock.

A moment later the cycling light flashed on and Jan could hear the air pumps labouring. He swung about to face the lock, floating there, waiting expectantly as the green light blinked and the inner door opened.

'Raise the hands. Don't move.'

Jan did as he was ordered and two armed men kicked in from the lock chamber. One of them ignored Jan and swung on by him towards the Captain who turned his abuse in the newcomer's direction. The other man, his face obscured by the gold sputtering of his helmet, waved his gun towards the airlock.

'Get into one of those suits,' he said.

While Jan was putting it on the first man came down from the control room. 'Just the two of them,' he said.

'And maybe a bomb wired to go off. This still could be a trap.'

'Well you volunteered for this mission.'

'Don't remind me. Stay with the tied up one, don't release him, while I shuttle this one over.'

Jan was only happy to obey. Once outside the lock he saw the spidery form of a medium-sized deep spacer in orbit to the rear of the scout. His captor, with a jet pack on his suit, grabbed Jan by the arm and towed him over to the open airlock of the waiting ship. There were two other gunmen watching him as he came out of the airlock and stripped off his suit. A large man in a black uniform was looking at him closely. His hair was blond, melting into gray, his jaw large and pugnacious and thrust in Jan's direction.

'I am Admiral Skougaard,' he said. 'Now tell me what all this is about.'

133

Jan was unable to talk, speechless, overwhelmed by a sense of deepest despair.

Because the Admiral was wearing the same Space Forces uniform that he was.

# Chapter Sixteen

Jan fell back, as though struck a physical blow. The guns followed him and the Admiral frowned at the movement – then nodded understandingly.

'The uniform, is that it?' Jan could only nod wordlessly in return. The iron face cracked into a grim smile. 'Perhaps I wear it as you do – if you are what you say you are. Not all men of Earth are traitors to mankind. Some of us helped, or there would have been no rebellion from the stars. Now I am going to have you searched, Kulozik, and then you will tell me your entire story in the finest detail that you can.'

The Admiral was no fool and made Jan repeat the details over and over, checking on names and dates and many precise points that he seemed familiar with. They were interrupted just once when a report came in that the IP-256 had been searched for bombs and other devices and was clear. A pilot would take her to join the fleet. Finally the Admiral raised his hand and cut Jan short.

'Niels,' he ordered. 'Get us some coffee.' He turned back to Jan. 'I am going to accept your story – for the time being. All of your details about the food expedition are correct, including some that I doubt the Earth forces could know. I am aware of the true facts because I was the one who gathered the ships and arranged all the organization of the expedition.'

'Did any of them get through?'

'Over half. Not as many as we hoped, but enough to ward starvation off for a while longer. Now we come to the new and interesting part of your story and frankly, I have just no way to evaluate it. You know this Thurgood-Smythe well?'

'Far too well. My brother-in-law as I said. He is a monster of cunning.'

'And treachery. We can be absolutely sure of that. He is either betraying his trust and aiding the rebellion. Or has laid a complex and treacherous trap to destroy us. So it must be treachery either way.'

Jan sipped the strong, black coffee and nodded agreement. 'I know. But what can we do? At least one part is certain, the Israeli participation.'

'Which could simply be a more deadly part of the trap. To lure us in and destroy us. The Israelis could very well be helpless pawns, doomed to destruction to further his ends.'

'They might very well be. It is the sort of thing that would appeal to him. I hadn't thought about that. But what of his plan to seize the Mojave base? That sounded reasonable. It certainly would affect the outcome of the war.'

The Admiral laughed, then blew on his coffee to cool it. 'Not only reasonable, but the only possibility of victory for either side. We know it and they know it. We could capture the Lunar bases, the satellites, even all of the Lagrange colonies, and Earth could survive. Her fleet would be as strong. And we would grow weaker with every passing moment. Mojave is the key. The other shuttle bases are merely landing strips. Whoever controls Mojave controls space operations – and wins this war.'

'Then it's that vital?'

'It is.'

'What do you plan to do?'

'Analyse it and sleep on it before I see you again. In any case there is nothing to be done yet, not until we are closer

136

to Earth's orbit. I'm going to lock you in a cell for a while. Sorry.'

'Don't be. After Captain Lastrup's company I'll enjoy the solitude. How is he?'

'Under sedation. He is in a bad way mentally and will need treatment.'

'I'm sorry about that.'

'Don't be. This is war. In the same situation he would undoubtedly have killed you.'

An aide interrupted with a printout which he handed to the Admiral, who read it slowly, then raised his eyes to Jan. And smiled as he extended his hand.

'Welcome aboard, Jan Kulozik. This is the confirmation that I was waiting for. One of our ships is in orbit around Halvmörk, unspaceworthy after the fighting. But its communication apparatus is operational and they are hooked into the Foscolo net. They have checked your story out with the people there. What you have told us is the truth. There is an additional message here that they confirmed all of the personal parts of your story with your wife. She sends her love.'

Jan seized the Admiral's outstretched hand. 'It's my pleasure to serve with you, sir. I've had no part in the rebellion up until now . . . '

'You have done more than most people. You are the one who saw to it that the corn was waiting when the ships arrived – it would have burned except for your leadership. Do you realize how many lives that food saved?'

'I know, I realize that it was important. But it was a passive action that's over and done with now. The reason that I was arrested and transported in the first place was because of my activities in the resistance. Now that the planets are free, and the last battle is about to begin, you must understand, I want to take a part in that.'

'And so you shall. Just as long as you make yourself

available at all times for our intelligence people. They'll want to pick your brain. Then we may need you as well for liaison with the Israelis once the fighting starts. Satisfactory?'

'Yes, of course. I'll do whatever is asked of me. By training I'm an electronic engineer and I used to specialize in microcircuitry design. But it has been mostly mechanical maintenance the last years.'

'That is first class – and there is a very good chance that you are just the man we need. I want you to meet another technician, Vittorio Curtoni. He is in charge of our armament, and has designed most of our defences, including what everyone refers to as the secret weapon. I understand there are still some teething troubles with it, so perhaps you could be of help.'

'That would be ideal.'

'Good. I'll arrange transport to the *Leonardo*.' The Admiral raised his hand and an aide came hurrying over.

One of the scouts vectored to the flagship while Jan suited up again, then transferred to it. He stayed in the open airlock so he would not waste any time pressurizing and depressurizing. Through the open hatch he could see the arc of deep spacers that spread out and away on both sides. One of the ships was coming close, growing larger and larger until they killed their momentum just a few metres away. Jan kicked out and drifted across the gap to the waiting and open airlock of the *Leonardo*.

A lean, black-haired man with a great brush of a moustache was waiting for him inside.

'Are you Kulozik, the one who is supposed to help me?' he asked, with more suspicion than enthusiasm in his voice.

'If you're Vittorio Curtoni, then I'm the one. Yes, I hope that I can help. I know I can if you can use the services of an experienced microelectronic engineer.'

Curtoni's wariness vanished instantly. 'Can I use you? Can a starving man use a grilled pig? Let me show you what we have been doing.' He led Jan deep into the ship, talking rapidly and scarcely stopping for breath.

'Jury-rigged, all of it, invented, manufactured and tested all on the same day. Sometimes. Admiral Skougaard, of course, a great help. Would have taken years instead of months if he hadn't turned over all the Space Forces blueprints and specs to us. He had been collecting them for a very long time, both the successful weapons and the proposals that were never carried through. What do you know about space warfare?' He lifted one quizzical eyebrow as he turned to face Jan.

'I've been in a space battle, but that was personal contact and hand to hand fighting. About battles between opposing forces – about all I know is what I see in the films.'

'Exactly! Films like this, I imagine.'

They entered a workshop, but Curtoni led Jan away from the machines and instruments to an ordinary TV set with a row of chairs before it. Curtoni keyed in a code and turned the set on.

'Sit, enjoy,' he said. 'This is an archaic film from the dawn of history that I found buried in the memory files. It is about a war among the stars, there – see!'

Music exploded from the loudspeaker and on the screen a mighty spacer flashed by. It had turrets and windows, gun emplacements and energy guns. Close behind was its pursuer, an even larger spaceship. Mighty rays and beams lashed out from the ships, lights flashed and there was the constant roar of engines, the zapping and crashing of the rays. There was a quick cut to a man in a turret, wheeling it about to fire his ray guns as the other ship swooped close. Luckily the smaller ship darted aside in time and fled for safety behind a nearby moon. Then the screen went blank and the roars and music died away.

'What do you think about that?' Curtoni asked.

'Very little. Seemed like fun, though.'

'*Merda!* Fun for infants in arms perhaps. But technically it is a monstrosity. Not one fact – not a single one – is scientifically correct. There is no sound in space, ships do not stop or turn suddenly, human reflexes are worthless in spacecraft manoeuvring or warfare, ray guns do not work . . . '

'I'll give you all that. I suppose I never really thought about it before. But don't dismiss the rays so quickly. I've worked with fusion cannon. They turn rock to lava in a few seconds.'

'Of course!' Curtoni held his hands out in the air, about a hundred centimetres apart. 'When the rock is this far away. What about a hundred metres away? Would it set fire to a piece of paper? Or a thousand kilometres, which is practically touching in space, when it would probably look like a light bulb if you could see it at all. The propagation of light, the propagation of any form of energy . . . '

'Of course, varies in proportion with the inverse square of the distance. I wasn't thinking.'

'Exactly! No one ever does until they are face to face with the problem. Which is why I show everyone my little training film first. It makes a point. Another point is that space war is so close to impossible that it can be called highly improbable.'

'But we're fighting one now, aren't we?'

Curtoni switched on the apparatus on one long bench and shook his head. 'We are fighting a rebellion, with Earth ships standing up to Earth ships. A real war, with ships from different civilizations coming from distant stars. Bunkum, like that thing we just saw. Even Earth's

Space Force never planned for a war. When hostilities began only a few of their ships had weapons. Installed but never used since the Commonwealth had absolute control of space and all of the spacers. They thought one or two might be seized some time so prepared their weapons just in case. And all of the same simple design. And what would that be?'

'Missiles obviously, adapted from those already designed for use in the atmosphere.'

'Perfectly correct. And how long do you think it would take us to design, develop and test our own missiles?'

'Years. Even if you captured some and copied them the manufacture of circuitry, control systems, jets ... probably just about as long.'

'Perfectly correct. It is a pleasure to speak with an intelligent man – that is of course someone who agrees with me. So we dropped the missile approach, though of course we have some on the Space Force ships that we took over. It was more important to develop defences first which we did by copying and modifying the Earth detection systems. We see the missiles coming, then generate electronic fields to mislead their guidance systems. For offence we have taken a more simple line. Like this.'

He picked up a small finned piece of metal from the bench and bounced it in his hand.

'That's a slug from a rocket pistol,' Jan said.

'Perfectly true. And a better weapon in space than it ever can be on a planet. No gravity to drop it, no air to slow it ... '

'Or guide it. The fins are useless.'

'Again you are right, Jan. It had to be redesigned with the thrust ahead of the centre of gravity. Very simple. Even simpler to mount a number of firing tubes on a turret and have the whole thing controlled by the navigation computer. Put a flock of these things into space in front of a spacer and you have a wreck. Speed equals mass and a few grams of metal will impact with tonnes of force. Good-bye enemy.'

Jan turned the tiny rocket over and over in his fingers. 'I do see one or two problems. Distance and speed, or rather they're both the same thing. You can't pack enough thrust into something this tiny.'

'Of course. These are mostly for defence. For attack we have developed this.'

He turned to the work bench and picked up a small metal ball, then pressed a button on the control board. Jan could hear a faint humming sound and when Curtoni held the sphere close to a vertical metal ring secured to the bench it sprang from his hand and hung, suspended, in the centre of the ring. There were other rings mounted close together down the length of the bench. When Curtoni pressed a second button there was a whistling sound and a flash and the sphere vanished. A loud crack echoed from the other end of the compartment as it crashed into the thick plastic sheet hung there and dropped to the deck.

'Linear accelerator,' Jan said. 'Just like the ones on the Moon.'

'Exactly the same. The large Lunar models take containers filled with ore and shoot them right out of the Moon's gravity, to the Lagrange satellite colonies for processing. As you see, a magnetic field is created in the first electromagnet ring. It suspends the iron sphere. Then, when the series of electromagnets are activated, they act as a linear motor, moving the sphere along faster and faster until it shoots out of the far end.' He turned and picked up a larger sphere that nestled comfortably in his hand.

'This seems to be the most practical size we have discovered by trial and error. It weighs a little under three kilograms, which is almost exactly six pounds in one of the more archaic systems of measurement. When I was researching this project I was helped a good deal by early ballistic texts that dealt with muzzle velocities and like terms. I was fascinated to find out that primitive sea battles were actually fought with solid shot of just this weight. History has many lessons for us.'

'How far have you gone with the project?' Jan asked.

'Four deep spacers have been converted to cannon ships. This is one of them. Named after one of the earliest theoreticians of the science who made such incredible drawings of his weapons. Leonardo da Vinci. We have loaded these ships with hundreds of thousands of cannon balls which have been forged in space from satellite iron. Most easily too. The specified mass of molten iron is released in free fall, whereupon its surface tension forms it into a perfect sphere. The secret weapons run the length of the ships and project from each end. The entire ship is rotated to aim the cannon, with aiming and firing controlled by the navigation computer. It all works well except for one small fault.'

'What's that?'

'Bugs in the control circuitry. The spheres must be launched within microseconds of each other to be effective. But we haven't been able to do this yet.'

Jan threw the cannon ball back onto the bench and smiled. 'Let me see your documentation and your diagrams and I'll do my best to get rid of your bugs.'

'Instantly! You will win this war for us yet!'

# Chapter Seventeen

'The fruit is ripe for harvesting,' the old man said. 'The longer we leave it the more we will lose.'

'There are a lot more important things you can lose,' his daughter said. 'Like your head, maybe. Come on Tata, the others are all waiting.'

The old man sighed with resignation and followed her out to the kibbutz truck. He was the last one to arrive and the others pushed over to make room for him on the crowded wooden benches. The firebox had been loaded with resinous pine logs an hour earlier so there was a good head of steam. As soon as he had the signal that they were all aboard, the driver opened the throttle and they moved out. Past the buildings where the lights still burned warmly, and down the winding lane through the orchards and out onto the main road. They drove in darkness, but the smooth surface was easy to see in the dim light from the star-filled sky.

They crossed the Syrian border a little after midnight, the transponder in the truck answering the request from the detection circuits with its identification code; the computer in Tel Aviv made a note of its departure. Just before they reached El Quneitra the truck turned into a deep wadi that wound back from the road. The darkness was intense between its high walls and the driver felt his way along, stopping suddenly when a light blinked ahead. There were camels waiting here and murmured guttural greetings as the passengers disembarked. The driver waited in the cab as they went by, some of them reaching up to pat his arm, other murmuring a few words. When they had all vanished in the darkness he reversed out and drove the truck back to the empty buildings of the kibbutz, reaching there just before dawn. He was the volunteer who was staying on.

'Like a city of the dead when I came through on the way here,' the painter said. 'A very frightening proposition to one of any imagination at all. Streets empty of children, only a few vehicles moving, one or two other pedestrians. It was dusk and the lights were coming on in the houses which at first I found very cheering. That is until I looked into the windows of one as I passed and saw that it was empty. It was the computers doing it, and I felt even more uncomfortable. Hold that corner of the stencil tight, if it's not asking too much, Heimyonkel.' He swung the spray gun back and forth with practised skill. 'When do you go?'

'Tonight. The family is already out.'

'Kiss your wife for me and tell her to think of a lonely bachelor in her dreams, alone and preparing for destiny among the shadowy hangars of Lod Airport.'

'You volunteered.'

'So I volunteered. That doesn't mean I have to be laughing with joy does it? All right, take it down.'

The painter stepped back and admired his work. On both swelling sides, and the wings, of the Anan-13 heavy transport the six-pointed star of Israel had been painted over. In its place was a starkly black cross.

'Symbolic, and not too nice,' the painter said. 'If you read history, which you don't, because you're a *yould*, you would recognize that cross. Do you?'

Heimyonkel shrugged and poured silver paint carefully into the spray gun.

'It's the cross of Germany, that's what it is, obliterating the *Mogen David* of Israel. Which is not nice and also, I wonder what the hell it is supposed to mean. Does the government know what it's doing? I ask you but you don't know and, P.S., I don't know either.'

Large sheets of paper were fastened into place with tape to cover the new insignia. After this had been painted silver there was nothing visible at a distance to indicate that the work had been done.

Amri Ben-Haim was very worried. He sat slumped in his favourite chair, staring at nothing, while the glass of lemon tea grew cold before him. Only when the sound of an approaching helicopter drew his attention did he sit up alertly and look towards the door. He sipped some of the tea and wrinkled his lips with displeasure. As he put it down Dvora came through the door with a package.

'Another one, and delivered by a Security policeman as well. Made my flesh crawl. He just smiled when he handed it over and wouldn't say a word.'

'Reflex sadism,' Ben-Haim said, taking the thick envelope from her. 'He can have no idea of its contents. Those kind of people just enjoy making others suffer.' He shook out the familiar sealed metal box and tapped out the combination. When it snapped open he took the disc it contained and put it into the computer. Thurgood-Smythe's unsmiling features appeared in the screen.

'This is our final communication, Ben-Haim,' he said. 'By now your troops and planes will be ready to begin the operation as instructed. The exact date will be given to you later this month, and you have your departure and flight plan. You will be flying in darkness all the way, so that will take care of visual and satellite observation. You have your instructions about the radar nets. Never forget that this is a coordinated attack and exact timing is the only way to prevent disaster.'

Thurgood-Smythe glanced down out of sight of the camera and smiled very slightly.

'I have a number of reports here that inform me that you seem to be moving a great deal of your population out of the country at night. Very wise. There is always the chance of a nuke or two, even if things go perfectly. Out of spite you might say. Or perhaps it is that you don't trust me? Nor should you have reason to. Nevertheless you are taking the correct course of action and victory is its own reward.

'I hope to be at Spaceconcent in Mojave when you arrive. Do arrange with your troops not to have me shot, if you don't mind. Goodbye then, Amri Ben-Haim. Pray for success in our ventures.'

The image vanished. Ben-Haim turned away from the screen shaking his head. 'Don't shoot him! I'll flay him alive if anything goes wrong with this plan!'

Fryer panted heavily as he dragged his bad leg up the stairs, climbing a single step at a time. He carried the gun over his shoulder in order to leave one hand free to clutch onto the bannister. It was a hot, close day, and sweat cut runnels through the dust on his face. The boy struggled along behind him with the heavy case of grenades.

'In here,' Fryer said, opening the door carefully and looking in first to be sure that the curtains were still closed. 'All in order, my lad. Put them there under the window and go on about your business. I'll give you ten minutes to get clear. Go slow and don't get stopped at any checkpoints. If you do it will get into the London computer that you were in this area and that will be the end of you.'

'Can't I stay, Fryer? I could help, help you get away too with that bum leg.'

'Don't worry, lad, they won't get the old Fryer. They

got me once, right and proper, gave me this leg and a tour of the camps in the Highlands. Once was more than enough of that, let me tell you. I'm not going back. But you're getting out, now, and that's an order.'

Fryer sat down on the case with a wheeze of relief and listened to the footsteps retreating back down the stairs. Good. One less thing to worry about. He dug out a joint, thin and black and almost pure hash. A few good lungfulls had him feeling better so that he didn't even notice the pain in the leg. He smoked slowly and carefully, and waited until the roach was burning his lip before he spat it out, grinding it under his heel into the plank floor. Then he drew the curtains aside and carefully lifted open the window. A light breeze blew in from Marylebone, carrying with it the sound of heavy traffic. A military convoy was passing and he drew back against the wall until it had gone by. When the sound had dwindled and vanished he pulled open the lid of the case. Taking out one of the grenades he bounced the chunky cylinder in his palm. Made by hand from scrap metal, shaped and filed and loaded with care. When he had tested the gun out in the wasteland only one in twenty had misfired. And they had improved the things since then he had been told. He hoped so. Holding the gun with the base down he let the grenade slide down the tubular barrel. It hit the bottom of the barrel with a solid chunk. Good. Fryer leaned forward and looked across the road at the grey cliff of Security Central.

Not a window broke the grim facade. The headquarters of Security in Britain, and now possibly the whole world. A prime target. If the calculations were correct the launching charge should be just enough to put the thing onto the roof of the first setback on the front of the building. Only one way to find out. Fryer put the gun to his shoulder, aimed carefully and squeezed the trigger.

The gun cracked and the butt smacked him hard in the shoulder. He saw the black speck arc up and over the edge. Perfect. Another grenade dropped down the barrel and when he fired this time he saw white smoke beginning to billow up from the roof of the setback.

'Well done, me old son,' he said cheerfully, then put round after round as close to the same place as he could. The thermite in the grenades would burn through anything, that's what the boffin had said. He was absolutely correct.

Alarms were going now and armed men were beginning to appear in the street below. Fryer drew back from the window so they couldn't see him, then lay prone on the floor and continued to fire from that position.

The next time he pulled the trigger there was only an angry hiss from the gun.

'Bloody hell!' he muttered savagely as he rolled over and inverted the gun to bang the muzzle on the floor. The misfired grenade slid out and dropped free, smoking and sputtering. He clutched at it, grabbed it up cursing at his burnt hand, then threw it through the window. There was an explosion just below followed by screams of pain.

Serve the bastards right, he thought, getting too close. He scrambled to the door, ignoring the pain in his hand, and fired the next one down the stairwell. There were more shouts and a spray of bullets that passed over his head. That would keep them busy for a bit.

There were only two grenades left when they broke the door down. He fired one of them at the attacking men and was reaching for the very last grenade when the bullets tore through him. He died quickly, lying on his back under the window, looking up at the clouds of smoke blowing by outside.

# Chapter Eighteen

Admiral Comrade Kapustin felt very secure, very secure indeed. He whistled lightly through his teeth while he pulled his high leather boots on, then stood and smoothed down his tunic before the mirror, pulling at it so it bloused out nicely above the wide leather belt. The rows of medals and decorations clinked gently when he strode to the door and threw it open. There was a clatter and a stamp as the marine guard outside drew himself up to attention. The Admiral touched his fingertips idly to the visor of his cap to return the salute as he strode by. The great day was here at last! His heels slammed into the deckplates even more heavily than usual so that his spurs jingled lightly. If anyone saw anything incongruous in boots and spurs in a spaceship, 200,000 miles from the nearest horse, they made no comment. The fate of anyone who dared to even smile in the direction of Admiral Comrade Kapustin was too awful to even consider.

When he entered the War Room the Admiral's aide, Onyegin, was ready as always. Clicking his heels and bowing slightly as he held out the silver tray. The Admiral downed the little glass of frigid vodka in a single gulp, then took one of the papirossi cigarettes; the aide produced a burning wooden taper to light it.

'Today is the day, Onyegin,' the Admiral said, expelling a cloud of aromatic smoke. 'The first space battle in history will be taking place soon, and I shall be the first officer to ever win one. A place in the history books. Any change in their course?'

'None, Comrade Admiral. You can see for yourself.'

He snapped orders at the Tank operator who activated the hologram field to show the course of the approaching enemy fleet. The Admiral stamped over to stand before the glowing display. It occupied a space of almost thirty cubic metres, taking up the entire centre of the War Room. The display was of course three dimensional and could be viewed from any side. A group of glowing symbols sprang into view in the tank, terminating in a dotted white line that ran up and out of sight.

'Their course so far,' Onyegin said, 'and the projection into the future.' A second broken line of light, this time red, extended down from the enemy fleet to end at floor level.

'Good,' the Admiral grunted. 'Now where will this take them?'

The small blue sphere of the Earth snapped into existence, surrounded by her captive satellites and orbiting Moon. The line of the course passed them all by.

'That is the projection as of this moment, not taking into consideration any future changes,' Onyegin said. 'However there are still course alterations possible. Like this.'

The red line fanned out into a number of arcs, each one of them terminating at one of the objects in space. The Admiral grunted again.

'Earth, the Moon, power satellites, colonies, anything. Well that's why we are here, Onyegin, learn that lesson. We defend Earth. Those criminals must pass us to work their mischief, and that will not be an easy thing to do. And my old friend Skougaard is leading them. What a pleasure! I shall personally execute the traitor when he is captured. Vodka!'

He downed another glassful, then seated himself in his command chair where he had a perfect view of the Tank, the pickup microphone beside his head swivelling automatically to follow his every move.

'The fighting so far has been sordid, just filthy stabs in the back. Bombs and mines and treachery. They have not only been traitors, but cowards as well who have fled our wrath, then sent us packing with missiles from planetary bases. That is all over now. We have had enough time to lick our wounds, to organize and regroup. Now we are on the defensive and they must come out and meet us. What a shock they will get when they do that. Let me see the latest photographs.'

The astronomers on the Earth-orbiting, 13 metre optical telescope had protested when ordered to photograph the approaching fleet. Their enormous metal reflecting mirror was designed for completely different purposes, they said. Shielded from the sun, with no atmosphere to dim its vision, it could penetrate the mysteries of the incredible distant galaxies, examine closely the separate star systems thousands of light years beyond our own. Important research was in progress; this was no military toy to spy out invaders. Their attitude had changed abruptly when a score of Security men had arrived on the next shuttle from Earth. Ways were found to look at the attacking fleet.

The rebel spacers filled the tank now. Fuzzy and grey, but still distinct, stretched out in a long arc.

'The flagship, the *Dannebrog*,' Admiral Kapustin ordered.

The ship in the centre of the attacking line swelled up until it was a metre across, fuzzy and unclear, just its outline distinct enough to see.

'Is this the best you can do?' The Admiral was displeased.

'We have been doing some computer enhancing,' Onyegin said. He did not add that most of the enhancing had been done by letting the computer see a photograph of the flagship. The three dimensional image blurred, changed and cleared. An apparently solid image now floated there.

'Better,' the Admiral condescended. He walked over and stabbed his finger into it. 'I have you Skougaard, you and your precious *Dannebrog*. You shall not escape. Now, let me have a display of our converging courses.'

The image changed again – with the symbols of the enemy fleet at one side of the Tank, the Earth forces on the other. First a broken line sprang across the Tank from the invaders, then one from the defenders. Where the two lines intersected sets of numbers appeared, one green, one yellow. The last digits flickering and changing constantly. Green represented the distance in kilometres to the intersection from their present position, yellow the time to get there at their present speed. The Admiral studied the figures closely. Still too far.

'Show me ten and ninety.'

The computer made the complex calculation in microseconds and two arcs of light cut across their future course, less than a quarter of the way to the enemy fleet. The arc closest to the fleet was the 90, a range at which 90 per cent of their missiles could be expected to strike the enemy – if no evasive or screening action was taken. The 10 was further out and represented 10 per cent of the missiles. There were hours to go before even this impractical range would be closed. Space warfare, like ancient naval warfare, consisted of long journeys punctuated by brief encounters. The Admiral sucked happily on his cigarette and waited. He had always been a man of infinite patience.

Skougaard's flagship, the *Dannebrog*, did not have an overly sophisticated War Room like its opposite number, the *Stalin*. Skougaard liked it that way. All of the information he needed was visible on the screens, and if he wanted a larger image a projection apparatus threw a picture that could cover the entire wall. It was all solid state, with multiple parallel circuitry, so there was very little that could go wrong. Any force strong enough to incapacitate the circuits would undoubtedly destroy the ship as well. The Admiral always felt that a complex hologram display, with its intricate circuitry, was just wasted effort and unnecessary complication. Since the machines did all of the work they only needed to show him what was happening in the simplest manner, then obey his instructions the instant they were given. He looked at the displays of the converging fleets and rubbed his large jaw in thought. He finally turned to Jan who waited quietly at his side.

'Then my heavy weapons are in perfect working order, ready for operation at any time. Good. I have a feeling of some reassurance now.'

'The problem was not too complex a one,' Jan said. 'If the truth be known I applied some of the work I had done on automated production lines where we have had to speed up repetitive work. It is a matter of thinking mechanical and not electronic. Feedback cycles are fine in circuitry because the various operations happen so fast that they appear instantaneous in real time. But with mechanics you are moving physical objects that have both weight and mass. You can't stop and start them as easily, and when you do it takes measurable amounts of time. So I rewrote the cannon ball loading program in units, so that each one of the cannon balls was constantly in motion and controlled by a file in the program all on its own. Therefore if there should be a mishap or a slowdown, that particular cannon ball is shunted aside and the next one takes its place. There will be no complete shutdown and restart as you had in the past. It also means that the cannon balls can be fired at much shorter intervals, which will allow the interval between firings to be exactly regulated.'

The Admiral nodded appreciatively. 'Wonderful. And since time means distance in an orbit we can space them out exactly. How close together can they be fired?'

'The best we can do is one about every three metres.'

'Your best is incredible. That means I can fire across the line of approach of a ship or a fleet and they will run into a solid wall of those things.'

'Ideally. This will simplify the range function leaving only aim to worry about.'

'I have some surprises in store for my old friend, Kapustin,' the Admiral said, turning back to the screens. 'I know him very well, his tactics and his armaments – and his stupidity. While he has no idea what I am going to hit him with. This is going to be an interesting encounter. I think you will find it something worth watching.'

'I don't imagine that I'll have much time to be a spectator. I thought I would be with the gunners.'

'No. You will be more valuable here with me. If Thurgood-Smythe contacts us, or if there is any situation involving his presence, I want you here to evaluate it instantly. He is the only unknown factor in my calculations. Everything else has been allowed for. The computations made, the program written.'

As though to drive home the point the numbers on the course screen began to flash and a horn sounded. 'Course change,' the computer annouced aloud at the same time. The vibrations of the engines could be felt through the soles of their feet.

'Now we will see how fast Kapustin's computer is,' Skougaard said. 'Also, how fast he is himself. A machine can only supply information. He will have to make up his mind what to do with it.'

'What's happening?' Jan asked.

'I am splitting my forces. For two very important reasons. This ship, and the *Sverige* over there, are the only ones that have sophisticated anti-missile missiles – for the simple reason that they are both deserters from the Earth Space Forces. Old Lundwall, who commands the *Sverige,* should have retired a decade ago, but he is still the best there is. He and I worked out this operation together. We will each head a squadron of ships lined up in a file behind us. There is a good reason as well for this. While I know that our people have worked very hard on electronic systems of missile avoidance, I would rather rely in the beginning on known technology. I am sure that these systems will work well and there will be plenty of opportunity to use them later on. But if I have a choice, there is something very satisfactory in having a screen of seeker missiles out in front to soak theirs up before they can reach our ships.'

Jan watched the screens that displayed the positions of the various ships. They were slowly moving in relation to each other, in a complex pattern controlled by the computers. The flagship had drawn ahead, while half of the ships were moving into station behind it. The other half were doing the same with the *Sverige* – while at the same time both squadrons were separating as their courses diverged.

'That will give Comrade Kapustin something to think about,' Skougaard said. 'All of our ships are falling into line behind these two leading battleships. And that line will always be pointing at the enemy fleet. Which means that, as far as they are concerned, all of the ships except two will have disappeared. It's a good thing that the comrade does not read history. Have you ever heard of Admiral Nelson, Jan?'

'I have – if he's the chap who stands on top of the column in Trafalgar Square.'

'The very one.'

'Some early English hero, from the middle ages or something. Fought the Chinese?'

'Not quite. Though he would have probably enjoyed it. He must have done battle with every other navy. His greatest victory, a victory that killed him, was at the Battle of Trafalgar where he broke through the French line of ships just as I plan to do now. He had different reasons for doing so, though our result will be the same. The lead ship will bear the brunt of the fighting until the line is breached ...'

'Missiles launched,' the computer said.

'Aren't we out of range yet?' Jan asked.

'Very much so. But these are the anti-missile missiles. Their engines fire just a short blast then cut out. That means they form a protective umbrella out in front of us, to intercept the other missiles when they come. We also get some early warning that way.'

A short time later a sphere of soundless fire blossomed and grew in space far ahead of them. Distant as it was it was still bright and the visual screens went dark as they overloaded and the filters cut in.

'How very unusual,' Skougaard said. 'Kapustin is using atomic missiles in his first attack. A good idea, I suppose, if the tactic works. Very wasteful if it doesn't because I know just how many he carries.'

Admiral Skougaard looked at the time, then at the screen that displayed the two squadrons now lined up in straight lines astern of the leading ships.

'An historical moment,' he said. 'The beginning of the first battle of the first war in space. May it end in a victory for our forces. The entire future rests upon its outcome.'

# Chapter Nineteen

'He's up to something,' Kapustin said, concern but not worry in his voice. His trap was prepared. All that Skougaard could do was fall into it. In the Tank the ships of the enemy fleet were coming together, blinking out of sight one by one, until apparently only two remained. While the holograph presented a three dimensional image, all it had now was a two dimensional picture to work with.

'They are going into space drive!' Kapustin shouted. 'Trying to escape me!'

'That cannot happen, Admiral Comrade Kapustin,' Onyegin said, formulating his words carefully before he spoke. The hardest part of his job was giving the Admiral information in such a way that he could imagine he had thought of it himself. 'You were the one who first explained to me that because of the interlocking gravity fields the Foscolo space drive could not be used this close to a planet. Something far simpler is happening. They are forming two lines astern ... '

'Obviously. Any fool can tell that. Do not waste my time by explaining the obvious. But have you noticed that their courses have changed as well? Keep your eyes open, Onyegin, and you will learn one or two things.'

It was hard not to be aware of the number of changes taking place as the flashing arrows rotated and changed positions, the displayed numbers changing as well. While this was happening the Tank operators took time to program in two lines of ships in the Tank. It meant nothing but would please the Admiral. Which was always their first order of priority.

'I want some predictions where these new courses are taking them. And fire some missiles, atomic ones. They'll be wetting their drawers when they arrive.'

'A limited supply ... rather early don't you think ... perhaps other missiles ... '

'Shut up and do as ordered.'

The words were quiet and toneless and Onyegin went cold, knowing he had overstepped himself. 'Of course, instantly, a logically perfect idea!'

'And give me some predictions where these new orbits are heading.'

Curving cones of light appeared in the Tank, emanating from the two approaching squadrons. At first the cones engulfed great areas of space, including the entire Earth and a number of satellites. As further information came in from the radar sweeps the cones narrowed, shrinking to two lines again once the orbit changes had been made.

'Two separate strikes,' Kapustin said, glancing back and forth from one to the other. 'The first aiming at our Lunar bases. Fine. The missile batteries there will destroy them as they come close. And the other, where is it going?'

'Apparently towards geostationary orbit. There are any number of satellites out there. It could be ... '

'It could be anything. And it doesn't matter. They'll be dead and dispersed into thin atomic gas long before they get there. We'll divide our forces as well. I want both squadrons to intercept, cut directly across the course of those ships. They will have to get through us to attack Earth and that will be no easy thing.'

It was a battle of invisible forces, electrons in computers – light waves and radio waves in space. Neither of the opposing fleets could see each other visibly yet; this might never happen even after battle was joined. They were still thousands of miles from each other. Though closing rapidly, their tiny gleaming images would be invisible against the burning stars, even to a watcher in space. Only the explosion of the atomic missile could have been seen. These sailors of the starways were the true descendants of the first seagoing navies where large guns reached out over the horizon to destroy an enemy that was completely out of sight.

Closer the opposing columns swept, and still closer, until in astronomical terms they had merged into a single object. They still could not see each other. Only their optical telescopes, fitted with electronic magnification, could produce visible images. Admiral Kapustin looked at the enlarged outline of the *Dannebrog* that now filled the screen; he nodded grimly.

'The second squadron will do as I do, fire when I do. There will be no independent command. Nor will any other ships attempt to approach the *Dannebrog* after she is gutted. She's my prey. Fire a scattered missile pattern. Shake them up.'

Aboard the *Dannebrog* Admiral Skougaard smiled and slapped his knee.

'Look at that fool,' he told Jan, pointing to one of the displays. 'Spending his irreplaceable missiles like pocket money.' The computer kept a running tally of all enemy missiles destroyed or averted. 'Basically he is just a stupid man with no idea of tactics. I imagine he thinks that he can beat us by the use of brute force. Which could be possible if he waited until we closed, then our defences could be overwhelmed and beaten down by sheer numbers of missiles. However we have a few surprises in store so that tactic will not work either.'

'Main cannon firing has commenced,' the computer said.

Though the central axis of the line of ships was pointed at the opposing squadron, it was angled towards the invisible track in space down which the enemy was moving. The two big gun ships were pointing at that track – and they now began firing. Two continuous streams of iron spheres hurtled outwards towards the point in space where the enemy would soon be. Stern jets flared on the gun ships to keep them in position, to counteract the backward thrust of the cannon balls. The speeding streams of metal looked like pencils of light on the radar screen, moving so fast that they were soon out of sight. Only the blips of the defensive missiles remained, resembling a second and larger fleet moving ahead of them. Their radar reflectors, gauss fields and heat sources were designed to lead attacking missiles astray.

On board the *Stalin,* Kapustin was not as pleased as he should be.

'Are there technical errors? This cannot be true,' he said, pointing to the set of numbers that displeased him.

'There are always errors, sir,' Onyegin said. 'But they would be only a small percentage of the final figure.'

'Yet this stupid machine keeps telling me that there have been no hits on the enemy fleet. None at all. Yet with my own eyes I can see the explosions.'

'Yes, Admiral. But those are decoys to draw our fire. After each contact our monitoring missiles radar sweep the area of the explosion for debris. They can tell by the mass of debris whether a ship was destroyed – or another missile. But you must remember that with each explosion one of his decoys is destroyed. Since we have far more missiles than they have we will win in the end.'

Kapustin was slightly mollified, but not completely

pleased. 'And where are his missiles? Isn't the coward going to fire back?'

'Since he has a much smaller quantity, I imagine he will wait until the range has closed to exact the most value from them. But our defence screen is out there in front of us and will not be penetrated.'

The timing of the remark was most unfortunate. A moment after the words had left Onyegin's lips the alarms sounded. OBJECTS ON COLLISION COURSE was spelled out in letters of fire and screamed aloud at the same time. Almost instantaneously after this damage reports began coming in from ship after ship. The Admiral stared, horrified, at the vision screen that showed debris spraying from his spaceships; one of them exploded in a gout of flame as he watched.

'What is it? What is happening?' he shouted.

'Meteorite field . . . ' Onyegin said, though he knew that could not be possible.

The Admiral seemed paralysed by the disaster, sitting gape-jawed in his chair. Onyegin called for a display of what had caused the damage. Although the entire encounter had been over with in less than a second, the computer had recorded the action and now replayed it at slow speed. The first sign of approaching trouble was a wall or a bar that swept in from space across their track. It was at least two kilometres long and speeding with great precision in a collision course. Then the impact. It had to be enemy action. When a section was enlarged he could see that the apparently solid bar was made up of discrete units of matter. Gaps appeared in it as defensive missiles exploded, but it made little difference to the overall strength. It struck.

'It appears that there is a secret weapon,' Onyegin said.

'What is it?'

*A secret,* Onyegin was tempted to say, but not tempted very much since he greatly valued his life. 'Inert material of some kind that has been launched into orbit to meet us. What kind of material it is and how it projected to reach us is still unknown.'

'Will there be more?'

'I would presume so, though of course we cannot know. They might have expended all of their effort in their single try . . .'

'More defence missiles. Launch them instantly!'

'They seemed to have no affect at all the first time, Admiral. If we expend them now we will not have them later when we need . . .'

He fell, struck to the floor by Kapustin's open-handed blow. 'Are you disobeying orders? Are you interfering with my command of this fleet?'

'Never! I apologize . . . just advice . . . never happen again.' Onyegin pulled himself to his feet; a runnel of blood twisted across his face. 'Put out an umbrella of defence missiles . . .'

'All of them! This weapon must be stopped.'

Even as the command was uttered the missiles were launched. Onyegin wiped his sleeve across his mouth, smearing his uniform jacket with blood, unaware of it. What else could they do? There must be some action they could take, the fool of an Admiral was incompetent, the officers and men too much in fear of him to make any suggestions that might draw his attention to them.

'Might I suggest evasive action as well, Admiral. It could be more effective than the missile defences. Whatever the rebel's weapon is, it is unpowered, there were no radiations of any kind detected before it hit. Therefore it must be launched into its trajectory. If we altered speed there is a good chance the weapon would miss.'

'What – slow down? Do you take me for a coward?'

'No, sir. Of course not. Speeding up would have the same effect. Hurrying forward into battle.'

'Perhaps. Issue the order in any case. It can do no harm.'

'Cease firing with the big cannons,' Admiral Skougaard ordered. 'They've increased their speed so the last bombardment will miss, go behind them. But we made them suffer. Look at that screen. We seem to have hit a good quarter of them. The next barrage will finish them off. Are we in range of the small guns yet?'

'Coming up in thirty-two seconds, sir,' the ranging and aiming operator said.

'Commence firing then. I want a wall of iron out there for them to run into.'

The spiderweb turrets were in constant, minute and precise motion, pointing their tubular guns at the selected point in space. They were built of a simple array of girders upon which were mounted the launching tubes of the rocket guns. Flexible plastic tubes ran from the breach of each gun and back to the ship, carrying forward a continous supply of the small steel rockets. It was a crude, fast – but deadly efficient weapon.

When the measured point in space was reached, the firing circuits were actuated. Electronic ignition set off the rocket shell lodged in every breech. When these had hurtled away the next shells were moved into position, then the next. Since there was no need to lock and unlock the open breech, no shell casings to eject, the rate of fire was incredible, limited only by the mechanical speed of the loading magazine. In each gun an average of 60 rockets were pushed forward and fired every second, 480 from every turret. A total of 197 turrets had been built and installed in a feverish rush before the fleet had left, the final connections on many of them actually being completed en route. The effort had been worth it.

Every second 94,560 rocket slugs flamed out from the guns. Two and one third tonnes of steel. When the firing stopped at the end of one minute, over 141 tonnes of flying metal had been launched towards the Earth fleet. Corrections had been constantly made in the aim during the firing, including a computation that would allow for a certain amount of evasion by the enemy if they should fire their jets.

Outward, further and further the invisible mass sped, a sparkling fog on the radar screens that quickly vanished. The same computer that had aimed the missiles, now counted down towards their moment of arrival. First the minutes, then the seconds, hurrying steadily backward towards zero. Now!

'My God . . . !' Jan gasped as the optical screen lit up with the multiple explosions. All of the defensive missiles had been activated at approximately the same moment by the mass of steel. Space was on fire with atomic and chemical blasts, clouds of flame that expanded and merged as though to screen the destruction and tragedy that was happening behind it.

As the attackers sped past the still growing cloud they could see the enemy fleet. Admiral Skougaard had his guns aimed and missiles ready. After one glance he ordered them to stand down. He turned in silence from the screen; he had known most of the men who had died; they had been his comrades.

Where once a fleet of space ships had been there now existed only torn and jumbled metal debris. Mixed in with it was the exploded flesh of Admiral Kapustin along with that of every man who had sailed with him. The defensive fleet had ceased to exist, both squadrons destroyed in the same manner, within seconds of each other.

The two clouds of wreckage and fragments were quickly left behind.

Ahead lay Earth.

# Chapter Twenty

'I should be getting to my plane now,' Dvora said. 'All of the others are aboard.'

She had grown tired of sitting in the car and had climbed out to lean against its side. The night was warm, the stars flickering brilliantly in the rising air currents. Although the airport was blacked out, the dark silhouettes of the big transports were visible where they were lined up along the runway. Her ammunition bag, machine pistol and helmet were at her side. Amri Ben-Haim stood next to her, the bowl of his pipe a glowing spark in the darkness.

'There is no rush, Dvora,' he said. 'There are thirty minutes at least to take-off. Your soldiers are grown men, no need to hold their hands.'

'Grown men!' she sniffed expressively. 'Farmers and university professors. How well will they behave when there are real bullets coming their way?'

'Very well, I am sure. Their training has been the best. Like yours. You just have had some field experiences that they have not. Rely on them ...'

'Message coming through,' the driver said as his radio beeped for attention.

'Accept with my code identification,' Ben-Haim said.

There was a murmured interchange. The driver leaned out the window. 'A two word message. *Beth doar.*'

'Post office!' Ben-Haim said. 'They've done it. Taken out the Khartoum station. Tell Blonstein that the situation, to use his favourite expression, is go. Then get to your plane. You shouldn't be hanging around out here.'

Dvora had her helmet on, her microphone activated, the

message passed. 'Yes ... yes, General. I'll do that.' She turned to Ben-Haim. 'A communication for you from General Blonstein. He says to keep an eye on Israel for him. He'd like to find it here when he gets back.'

'So would I. When you talk to him next say I told you that was up to him, not me. I'll be sitting on my porch waiting for results. That is just as long as I have a porch to sit on.' Dvora gave him a quick kiss on the cheek and was gone, the sound of her running feet vanishing in the darkness towards the planes.

Ben-Haim watched quietly as, one by one, the engines of the massive planes burst into rumbling life. Exhausts spat tongues of flame that quickly died away as their throttles were adjusted. The first craft was already moving, picking up speed, faster and faster until it hurled itself into the air. The others were just seconds behind. Both runways were in use; a steady flow of rushing dark shapes that suddenly ended. The thunder of their engines diminished, died, and silence returned. Ben-Haim's pipe was dead; he tapped it against his heel to knock out the ashes. He felt neither sorrow nor elation, just a great weariness after the days of preparation and tension. It was done, the die cast, no changes were possible now. He turned to the car.

'All right. We can go home now.'

Out of sight in the sky above, the flight of planes circled out over the ocean as they gained height; the airspace over Israel was too small for such a manoeuvre. There was no concern about radar detection here, but there were settlements and towns in the adjoining countries where people might hear and wonder what all the planes were doing up there in the night sky. When they crossed Israel again they were over six miles high, their engines inaudible on the ground below. In a formation of two

168

stepped vees they turned southeast, flying down the length of the Red Sea.

Grigor looked out of the window of the plane and made tsk-tsk sounds with his tongue.

'Dvora,' he said, 'what I see is not strictly kosher.'

'A drove of pigs?'

'Not even with my eyesight from this altitude.' Grigor was a mathematician, very absent-minded, possibly the worst soldier in Dvora's squad. But he was a sharpshooter who never missed his target no matter what the pressure; an asset to be relied upon. 'It's where we are going. We're supposed to be attacking Spaceconcent in the western United States – I know, don't get excited. A big secret with the name removed from all the maps. A child could tell. Anyway, the North Star was very clear back there when we turned. So now we are going south so I wondered, something not quite kosher. Or these planes maybe have big fuel tanks to get to America by flying over the South Pole?'

'We are not taking the most direct route.'

'You can say that again, Dvorkila,' Vasil, the heavy weapons gunner, said.

They were leaning towards her from the seats in the front and in the back, listening.

'No secrets now,' another soldier said. 'Who can we talk to about it?'

'I can tell you about this part of our course,' she said. 'But no more until after we refuel. We are going south now, staying over the sea, but we'll be turning west very soon over the Nubian desert. There is – or rather there was a radar station in Khartoum – but that has been taken care of. It was the only one we had to worry about since there is not another one all the way across Africa, not until we get to Morocco . . . ' her voice died away.

'And then?' Grigor urged. 'Something maybe to do with

the big black cross I found on the side of this plane when I helped to tear the paper off it earlier tonight. Sailing under false colours like pirates?'

'It's top secret . . . '

'Dvora, please!'

'You're right, of course. It can't do any harm now. We have, what you might call, agents placed high up in the UN government.' Or maybe they have us, she thought to herself. No doubts now. Even if this was a trap they had to go ahead with it, right to the bloody end. 'So we know that German troops are being sent to help hold the space centre in Mojave. We have their identification and their markings on our planes. We intend to take their place.'

'Not so easily done,' Grigor said. 'I assume that there are other things that you are not telling us . . . '

'Yes. But I can add just one thing more. We are flying just one hour ahead of the German planes. That's why the delay on the take-off. Exact timing is very important, since once we're airborne we're out of touch with the ground. From now on everything happens by schedule. So – take some rest while you can.'

The dark map of Africa moved past slowly and steadily beneath them. Most of the men slept in the blacked out planes, only the pilots were alertly awake and watching their instruments, monitoring the operation of the automatic pilots. General Blonstein, a qualified flyer himself, was in the pilot's seat of the lead plane. From this height he could make out clearly the darkness of the Atlantic Ocean, coming into view beyond the pale deserts of Morocco. The receiver rustled.

'*Rabat tower to Air Force flight four seven five. Do you read me?*'

'Air Force flight four seven five. I read you, Rabat tower.'

The radio contact was just a formality. The ground

station had already activated the transponder in every craft, completely automatically, which had returned all the recorded data including identification, route and destination.

'*We have you cleared for the Azores, Air Force flight.*' There was the sound of mumbled voices for a moment. '*We have a flag on your flight plan that you seem to be running fifty-nine, that is five niner, minutes ahead of your filed flight plan.*'

'Strong tail winds,' Blonstein said calmly.

'*Understood, Air Force flight. Out.*'

There were other ears listening in on the ground control frequency. A burnoosed man concealed from sight in a grove of trees close to the coast highway. Parallelling the highway were the columns of a high tension electricity line. The man had been following the conversation closely, frowning as he concentrated on making out the words through the crackle of static on his cheap radio. He waited a few moments to be absolutely sure that the transmission was over. Nothing else followed. He nodded and bent down to press the button on the box at his feet.

A bright white flame lit up the night; a few seconds later the sound of the explosion reached him. One of the pylons in the 20,000 volt line leaned over, faster and faster, until it struck the ground. There was a colourful display of large sparks that went out quickly.

So did half the lights in Rabat. It was not by accident that the radio beacon station was included in this circuit as well.

The duty staff at Cruz del Luz airport on the island of Santa Maria were all soundly asleep. Very few planes had been stopping recently for refuelling in the Azores, so the night shift had quickly become used to staying awake during the daytime hours. Admittedly someone had set the alarm bleeper, but that wasn't really needed. The radio would wake them up.

It did. Captain Sarmiento was pulled from a deep and dream-free sleep by the amplified voice from the wall speaker. He stumbled over from the couch and banged his shins ruthlessly on the control station before he found the light switch.

'Cruz del Luz here, come in.' His voice was rough with sleep and he coughed and spat into the waste basket while he groped through the printouts on his desk.

'*This is Air Force flight four seven five requesting clearance for landing.*'

Sarmiento's scrabbling fingers found the printout even while the voice was speaking; yes the right one. 'You are cleared for approach on runway one. I have a reading you are locked in to landing control.' He blinked at a figure on the sheet, then looked up at the clock. 'Your arrival approximately one hour ahead of schedule Air Force flight . . .'

'*Tail winds,*' was the laconic reply.

Sarmiento dropped wearily into his chair and looked with disdain at his sleepy, shambling crew just entering the office. His temper burned strongly.

"Sons of whores! A major refuelling, the first in six months, a most important wartime occasion and you lie around like swine in a sty.'

Sarmiento continued enthusiastically in this manner while his staff hurried, hunch-shouldered, about their duties. This was good employment and they wanted to do nothing to jeopardize it.

The runway lights came on brightly as the fire engine raced along it to take position at the end of the runway. Out of the darkness the beams of landing lights speared in and the first of the arrivals thundered overhead to slap down to the runway's surface. One after another they landed, and once on the ground were guided automatically to the refuelling points. Every bit of the operation was computer controlled. Engines were cut and brakes applied at the proper spot. A TV camera rose up from each refuelling well and scanned the undersurface of the wing above, locating the fuel access port. Once identified and pinpointed the smoothly articulated arm could open the cover and insert the hose so that pumping could begin. Sensors in each tank assured that there would be no overflow or spillage. While this industrious robot activity was taking place all of the big planes remained dark and quiet, sealed tight. Except for the command ship. The door on this one opened, the entrance stairs ground out and settled into place. A man in uniform came quickly down them and strode firmly down the length of the refuelling stations. Something drew his attention to one of the pits, he bent over and looked close. His back was to the tower, the underpart of his body in shadow, the package that slipped from his jacket dropped into the well, unseen. He stood, brushed his clothing straight, then continued on towards the illuminated control tower.

Sarmiento blinked up at the officer and felt slightly grubby. The man's black uniform was pressed and smooth, the buttons and gold braid gleaming in the light. A maltese cross hung about his neck, there were decorations on his breast, a glass lens covered one eye. Sarmiento climbed to his feet, impressed.

'*Sprechen sie Deutsch?*' the man said.

'I'm sorry, sir, but I don't understand what you are saying.' The officer scowled, then continued in thickly accented Portuguese.

'I am here to sign the receipted form,' he said.

'Yes, to be sure excellency.' Sarmiento waved in the direction of the computer bank. 'But that will not be ready until all of the refuelling is complete.'

The officer nodded curtly, then strode up and down the office; Sarmiento found important work to do. They both turned when the bell rang and the completed form was ejected.

'Here, and here if you please,' Sarmiento said, pointing out the correct places, not even looking at the papers himself. 'Thank you very much.' He tore off the bottom copy and passed it over, happy to see the man turn and stamp away towards his waiting aircraft. Only when he was safely aboard did Sarmiento pick up the forms to file them. Strange names these foreigners had. Hard to read the angular script. Looked like Schickelgruber . . . Adolph Schickelgruber.

Urgent hands pulled the officer through the door, closing it almost on his heels.

'How much time?' he asked, urgently.

'About twenty-eight minutes yet. We have to get airborne before they make radio contact.'

'They might be behind schedule . . . '

'They could be ahead of it if our imaginary tailwind is real. We can't take any chances.'

The first planes were already off the runway, vanishing up into the night. The lead plane was the last one to go, following the others out into the darkness. But instead of reaching for altitude it made a long circle out over the ocean and returned to the air field. Throttled back, flying low, making a pass down the runway.

'There's the fire engine, back in the barn already,' someone said.

'And the rest of the men still in the building, no, there's one at the door, waving,' General Blonstein said. 'Let's give him a blink of our lights to say farewell.' This time they continued out across the ocean to the west. Blonstein pressed the earphones to his head, listening, praying for time. Still all right, nothing, no other calls yet. 'That's enough,' he finally said, flipping up a red cover and thumbing the button beneath it.

Sarmiento heard the strange thud and looked up at the window just as the column of flame jutted high into the air. The aviation fuel burned brilliantly. Alarms sounded on all sides, the printers chattered, the radio burst to life with prerecorded emergency messages.

The German troop carriers had just cleared the African coast when the message came through.

'New course,' the commander said, summoning up a map on the screen. 'Some sort of accident, message didn't go into details. Anyway, we're cleared now for Madrid.'

The commander was concerned about the new vector and the status of fuel in his tanks. He never thought to call through to Cruz del Luz airport; that was no concern of his now. Therefore the worried, frightened and tremendously upset Captain Sarmiento was spared one other problem in addition to the ones that now tormented him. He would not have to worry about how two flights that night had been scheduled to arrive with the same flight numbers and identical descriptions.

# Chapter Twenty-One

'That is the first half of the job completed,' Admiral Skougaard said with satisfaction as the debris of the enemy fleet vanished behind them. 'It went far better than I had hoped. Did as well as Nelson did at Cape Trafalgar, better if you consider the fact that I am still alive. And we suffered not a scratch, unless you count the man with a broken foot where one of our cannon balls dropped on it. Course corrections?'

'Computed, sir,' the operator said. 'Engines will be firing in a little over four minutes.'

'Excellent. As soon as we are in our new orbits I want the watches below to stand down and eat.' He turned to Jan. 'Privilege of rank; I'm having mine now. Join me?'

Food had been the farthest thing from Jan's mind up to that moment. But as the tension of the past hours drained away he realized that it had been a long time between meals. 'I'll be happy to join you, Admiral.'

The table was already laid when they entered the Admiral's private quarters, the chef himself putting the last of the food on the table. The Admiral and the chef exchanged some remarks in a guttural and incomprehensible tongue, laughing together at a throaty witticism.

'Smorgasbord,' Jan said, eyes widening. 'I haven't seen that since – why I don't remember when.'

'*Stor kolt bord,*' Admiral Skougaard corrected. 'The Swedish term has taken over in the popular mind, but it is not the same thing at all. We Danes enjoy our food. I always ship out with my larder full. Growing empty now,' he sighed. 'We had better win this war quickly. Here's to victory.'

They toasted each other with tiny glasses of frigid akvavit, downing them in a gulp. The chef instantly refilled them from the bottle – frozen into its own cake of ice on the table. Thickly buttered rye bread was heaped high with lashings of herring in endless variety. Cold beef with grated horseradish, caviar with raw egg, more and more and all washed down with bottles of cold Danish beer. Theirs was the appetite of victory – of survival as well. In defeating the enemy they had extended their own existences a bit more into the future. Eat and drink; the morrow would come soon enough.

Over coffee, with just enough room left to nibble a bit of cheese, their thoughts returned irresistibly to the final phase of the battle.

'Would you believe that I had the computer programmed for at least two dozen future plans, depending upon the outcome of the battle?' Skougaard said. 'And of all of them I came up with the best. Number one. So my next problem is how to keep that plan a secret from the enemy's reserves. Let me show you.'

He arranged the salt cellar, mustard pot, knives and forks upon the table top. 'Here we are, our squadron is the knife. Next to us is the fork, the second squadron. Over here is Earth and that is the way they are headed. The remaining enemy ships are in loose groupings, here and here. They'll be on interception orbits by now but they will be too late to interfere with what will happen next. Before they can reach this spot our ships will capture and occupy these spoons, the power satellites. As you know these big mirrors turn solar energy to electricity and radiate it to Earth as microwaves. This energy feeds the electric grids of Europe and North America, which means that they will be very unhappy when we cut it off. All of the satellites, at exactly the same second. With a little luck we'll start a blackout cascade. But all of this is really just nuisance value. Earth has enough other energy sources that they can cut in, so it won't matter at all in the long run. But the present is what concerns us. Hopefully they will try and dislodge our men. This will have to be done hand to hand because they don't dare fire missiles or they will destroy their own satellites. But we have no compunction about firing at their ships. It will be an interesting battle. And totally unimportant. A diversion, nothing more. Here,' he tapped the knife, 'is where they should be looking.'

The knife moved out and around one plate and back towards another which had some small cream cakes upon it. 'The Moon,' Skougaard said, touching the first plate. 'And Earth,' pointing to the second plate, then taking one of the cakes. 'Hopefully the diversion will pull off a lot of their defences. The second part of the plan should make a big hole in what is left.'

'This second part. This is where we coordinate with the attack on Spaceconcent in the Mojave desert?'

Skougaard licked a last bit of cream from his fingertips. 'Exactly. My hope is that with the destruction of their main fleet, the attack on the satellites, blackouts and power failures, resistance sabotage, why they just might forget about Mojave for the moment. If your friend – our friend hopefully – Thurgood-Smythe is telling us the truth, why he will have a lot to do with increasing the confusion. In any case, win or lose, we go for the big one.' He put a second knife beside the first one and moved them around the plate, to the back of the Moon.

'Here is where I divide my forces yet again. We will be out of sight and detection from the Earth stations when we are on the far side of the Moon. Also, when we pass this spot, here, we will be over the horizon and past the last remote detection station. That is when we fire our engines for a course change. A minor change for the main body of the squadron,' he moved one knife slightly away from the other, 'Since we don't want it to come out into the waiting missiles of the defence forces, which will be in position by that time. But a major change for the remaining two ships. This one and the troop transport. We change orbit and pile on the G's. We whip around the Moon like a weight on a string – and come out here. Far from the defences and on a precise orbit for Earth.'

'An orbit that will eventually terminate over the Mojave?'

'Exactly. The *Dannebrog* will supply cover, a missile umbrella screen against anything coming up from Earth. That should be easy because they have to rocket up out of the gravity well. We should have plenty of time to pop them off as they come. And we have nothing to fear from the Moon bases behind us since they will have had a few bombs and iron cannon balls down their throats to give them something else to think about.'

'You make it sound simple,' Jan said.

'I know. But it isn't. Warfare never is. You plan as best you can, then chance and the human factor come into it to produce the final results.' He poured a glassful of akvavit from the water-beaded bottle and threw it down his throat. 'A few more of these, then a good sleep – and we see what is waiting for us when we come out from behind the Moon. I suggest you get some rest as well. And if you are the praying type, pray that this strange brother-in-law of yours is really on our side this time.'

Jan lay down, but could not sleep. They were hurtling at incredible speed towards an unknown destiny. Dvora was mixed up in it; he should not be thinking about her, but he was. Halvmörk, all his friends and the rest of the people there. And his wife; they were light years away. Light years from his thoughts as well. This warfare, the killing, it was going to end soon. One way or the other. And Thurgood-Smythe, what about him? He was the deciding factor in the whole equation. Would his plan work – or was it just a convoluted and complex plot to betray and destroy them all? Warm flesh, dead flesh, guns, death and life, all swirled into a jumble and the alarm buzzer startled him awake. He had fallen asleep after all. The reason why he had set the alarm returned through the fog of sleep and a sudden knot of tension formed in his midrif. The battle was entering its final phase.

Jan found Admiral Skougaard in a philosophical mood when he joined him. Skougaard was listening to the muttered comments from the computers and nodding his head as he looked at the displays on the screens.

'Did you hear that?' he asked. 'The big cannons are firing again at a target they can't see, that will be destroyed well before they reach it. Have you considered the mathematical skill involved in this little exercise that we take so much for granted? I wonder how many years it would take us to do these computations by hand. Look –' he pointed at the cratered surface of the Moon slowly moving by beneath them. 'I supplied the computers with accurate photographic maps of the Moon. On these maps I marked the three missile bases that are located on the Earth side of this satellite. After that I simply instructed them to fire the cannon to knock these sites out. That is what they are doing now. In order to do this the Moon must be observed and our orbit, speed and altitude determined. Then the sites must be located in relation to this orbit. Then a new orbit must be calculated for the cannon balls, that will include our speed, their launching speed, and the precise angle that will permit their path to terminate on the chosen missile site. Marvellous.' His elation vanished as he looked at the time, to be replaced by the studied calm he presented during battle. 'Three minutes and Earth will be over the horizon. We'll see then what kind of reception is waiting for us.'

As Earth's atmosphere slowly rose into view the rustling static on their radios was replaced by muffled voices that became quickly clearer as they moved into the line of sight of the stations. The computers scanned all the space communication frequencies to intercept the enemy messages.

'A good deal of activity,' Skougaard said. 'They have been stirred up enough. But they have some good commanders left – all of them better than the late Comrade Kapustin. But if Thurgood-Smythe is doing his job there should be conflicting orders going out. Let us hope so since every little bit helps.'

The blue globe of Earth was clearly in sight now; a web of radar signals filled space, followed instantly by more accurate laser detectors once the rebels had been found. As soon as this happened the invading fleet broke radio silence and began searching and ranging as well. Figures and code symbols filled the displays.

'It could have been better for us,' Skougaard said. 'Then again it could have been a lot worse.'

Jan was silent as the Admiral called for course computations, estimates of closing speed, ranges, all of the mathematical details that were the essentials of space war. He did not hurry, although thousands of miles passed while he considered his decision. Once made it was irrevocable – so it had to be right.

'Signal to first squadron in clear. Plan seven. Then contact the second squadron, coded report.'

Skougaard sat back to wait, then nodded to Jan. 'The enemy has spread a wide web, which is what I would have done myself, rather than risking everything on covering a few orbital boltholes. They knew that we wouldn't come out from behind the Moon on the same orbit we were on when they lost contact with us. This is both good and bad for us. Good for the others in the first squadron. They are in tight orbit for two of the most important Legrange satellite colonies, the manufacturing ones. Whether they attempt to capture them or not depends entirely upon how hot the pursuit is. We'll know soon when all of the enemy course corrections are completed. It will be a slow stern chase because our opponent's forces are so widely separated. That could be dangerous for us because they could mass more ships than I would like to intercept us. Let us hope that they get their priorities wrong.'

'What do you mean?'

Skougaard pointed at the screen at the image of the troop carrier in orbit beside them. 'At this point in time everything depends upon that ship. Knock it out and we have surely lost the war. Right now its orbit terminates in central Europe, which should give the enemy something to ponder over. But during braking approach its course, and ours, will be changed to put us down in the Mojave. Just one hour after the Israeli attack begins. With our aid the base will be secured, the missile sites captured. When they are secured we can fight off any attack from space, or destroy the base if attacked by land. End of battle, end of war. But if they knock out that transport, why then we don't take the base, the Israelis will be counterattacked and killed – and we will have lost the war . . . wait. Signal from the second squadron.'

The Admiral read the report and grinned widely. 'They've done it! Lundwall and his men have taken all three power satellites.' The grin faded. 'They fought off the interceptors. We lost two ships.'

There was nothing to be said. Capture of these satellites, and the orbiting colonies, would be immensely important in ending the war quickly after Spaceconcent was taken. But right now both actions were basically diversions to split the enemy forces to enable the troop carrier to slip through. How successful these diversions would be would not be known until the Earth forces were established in their new courses.

'Preliminary estimation,' the computer said calmly. 'Eighty per cent probability that three ships will intercept force one alpha.'

'I was hoping for only one or two,' Skougaard said. 'I don't like the odds.' He spoke to the computer. 'Give me identification on those three.'

They waited. Although the approaching space ships could be clearly observed electronically, they appeared just as points in space. Until they could be seen as physical shapes the identification program had to look for other identifying signs. Degree of acceleration when changing course gave clues to their engines. When they communicated with each other their code identities might be discovered. This all took time – time during which the distance between the opposing forces closed rapidly.

'Identification,' the computer said. Skougaard spun to face the screens as the numbers appeared there far faster than they could be spoken aloud.

'*Til helvede!* he said in cold anger.' 'Something is wrong, very wrong. They shouldn't be there. Those are their heaviest attack vessels, armed to the teeth with every weapon that they possess. We can't get through. We're as good as dead now.'

# Chapter Twenty-Two

There was never any uncertainty about the summer weather in the Mojave desert. During the winter months conditions varied; there could be clouds, occasionally even rain. The desert would be uncharacteristically green then, dusted with tiny flowers that faded and died in a few days. Beautiful. That could not be said about the summer time.

Before dawn the temperature might drop down to thirty-eight degrees, what the Americans, still valiantly resisting the onslaught of the metric system, insisted on calling ninety. It might even be a few degrees cooler, but no more. Then the sun came up.

It burned like the mouth of an open oven as it cleared the horizon. By noon sixty degrees – one hundred and thirty – was not unusual.

The sky was light in the east, the temperature just bearable, when the planes came in to land. The tower at the Spaceconcent airfield had been in touch with the flight since they had begun to lose height over Arizona. The rising sun glowed warmly on their burnished skins as they dropped down towards the lights of the runway.

Lieutenant Packer yawned as he watched the first arrivals taxi up to the disembarkation points. Big black crosses on their sides. Krauts. The Lieutenant did not like Krauts since they were one of the Enemies of Democracy in the paranoid history books that he had been raised on. Along with Commies, Russkies, Spics, Niggers and an awful lot of others. There were so many bad guys that they were sometimes hard to keep track of, but he still managed to feel a mild dislike for the Krauts, even though he had never met one before. Why weren't there good American boys here, defending this strategic base? There were, his company among them, but Spaceconcent was international, so any UN troops might be assigned here. But, still, Krauts ... '

As the engines died the landing stairs slowly unfolded. A group of officers emerged from the first plane and came towards him. Soldiers clattered down behind them and began to form up in ranks. Packer had leafed through Uniforms of the World's Armies briefly, but he could recognize a general's stars without its help. He snapped to attention and saluted.

'Lieutenant Packer, Third Motorized Cavalry.' The officers returned the salute.

'General von Blonstein. Heeresleitung. Vere is our transportation?'

Even sounded like a Kraut from one of the old war movies. 'Any second now, General. They're on the way from the motor pool. We weren't expecting your arrival until ... '

'Tail vind,' the General said, then turned and snapped out commands in his own language.

Lieutenant Packer looked worried as the newly formed troops quick-stepped off towards the hangars. He moved in front of the General who ignored him until he worked up the nerve to speak.

'Excuse me, sir, but orders. Transportation is on the way – here are the first units now – to take your men to the barracks ... '

'Goot,' the General said, turning away. Packer moved quickly to get in front of him again.

'Your people can't go into those hangars. That is a security area.'

'It is too hot. They get in der shade.'

185

'No they can't, really, I'll have to report this.' He reached to turn on his radio and one of the officers rapped him hard on the hand with the butt of his gun. Then ground it into his ribs. Packer could only stare, speechlessly, and hold his bruised fingers.

'There is a silencer on that pistol,' the General said, all trace of an accent suddenly vanished. 'Do as I say or you will be shot instantly. Now turn and walk to that plane with these men. One word, a wrong action, and you are dead. Now go.' Then he added in Hebrew. 'Inject him and leave him there.'

When the last engine had been shut down the computer in the control tower disconnected the landing and taxiing program and shut it down as well, signalling that the operation was complete. One of the operators verified with a visual check using field glasses. All of the planes were wound down now. A lot of trucks and buses about; he wouldn't start clearing the ramps until they had moved out of the area. The convoy officer was going into a plane with two of the newcomers. Probably had a bottle in there. German soldiers were probably just like their American counterparts. Brawling, boozing and banging. Good thing they locked them behind wire most of the time.

'In the back, not here,' the Corporal said as the soldier opened the cab of the truck and started to climb in.

'Ja, Ja, gut,' the soldier said, ignoring the command.

'C'mon, Christ, I don't speak that stuff. In backski, fucking quickski ... ' He looked down in amazement as the newcomer leaned over and slapped him on the leg. Something stung. He opened his mouth to protest, then slumped forward over the wheel. The Israeli clicked the safety in place on the palm-hypo and put it into his pocket, then dragged the Corporal from behind the wheel as the door opened on the driver's side. Another Israeli slipped in, taking off his helmet and laying it on the seat beside him, then putting on the corporal's fatigue cap in its place.

General Blonstein looked at his watch. 'How much longer to go?' he asked.

'Three, four minutes, no more,' his aide said. 'Boarding the last coaches now.'

'Good. Any trouble?'

'Nothing important. A few people asking questions have been put to sleep. But we haven't hit any of the guarded gates or buildings yet.'

'And we're not going to until every one is in position. How much longer to jump-off?'

'Sixty seconds.'

'Let's go. These last people can catch us up. We're not going to change the attack schedule for any reason.'

Dvora sat next to Vasil who was driving the heavy lorry; her squad was jammed into the back. Her long hair had been tied into a bun and hidden under her helmet, her face was bare of any cosmetics.

'How much longer?' Vasil asked, his foot tapping the accelerator, the motor rumbling in response. She glanced at her watch.

'Any second now if they are keeping to plan.'

'This is a big place,' he said, looking up at the service towers, gantries and warehouses that stretched into the distance behind the wire fence. 'We can maybe take it – but we can't hold it.'

'You were at the last briefing. We're getting reinforcements to consolidate.'

'You never said where they were coming from.'

'Of course not. So if you're captured you won't be able to talk.'

The big man smiled coldly and patted the bandoleer of grenades hung about his neck. 'The only way they'll capture me is dead. So tell.'

Dvora smiled and pointed skyward. 'Help will come from there.' Vasi grunted and turned away.

'Now you sound like a rabbi,' he said, just as her radio sounded a rapid series of high-pitched bleeps.

'Go!' Dvora said, but he already had his foot down on the accelerator. 'Gunners ready?' she said into her radio.

'In position,' the voice said inside her head. She tightened her chin strap to keep the bone conduction headphone secured in place.

The big truck rolled around the corner of the warehouse and stopped by the military police box there. The gate that blocked the entrance remained shut. The MP leaned out and scowled.

'You're going on report, buddy, because you are stupid and you are also lost. That thing isn't cleared to come in here ... '

The time for harmless drug injections had passed. Through a slit cut in the canvas cover of the truck the muzzle of a machine gun emerged, firing, sweeping back and forth. Because of the long silencer on the end of the barrel it only made a muffled coughing sound; the crash of broken glass and punctured metal was much louder. A second gun on the other side killed the MP there.

'Ram it,' Dvora said.

The heavy truck lurched forward, crashing into the gate, pulling it down with a shriek of torn metal, drove over it. An alarm bell began sounding somewhere in the distance; there was the muffled sound of explosions.

Dvora had memorized their route, but she did not believe in taking chances so had the map unfolded on her lap. 'Left at the next corner,' she said, her finger on the track marked out in red. 'If we don't meet any resistance on the way this should take us directly to our target.'

The service road they were on cut through an area of

office blocks and warehouses. There was no other traffic. Vasil put his foot to the floor and the heavy truck picked up speed. The gearbox screamed as it shifted into top gear, the soldiers in back grabbing for support as they jarred through a pothole.

'That's the building we want, the big one . . . '

Her words ended in a gasp as the road surface ahead stirred and cracked, crumbled, then split from curb to curb. Vasil was standing on the brakes, the wheels locked, the tires screaming as they skidded, scarcely slowing, burning rubber. They looked on, horrified, braced themselves, unable to do anything else as they saw the concrete fall away in chunks and slabs as a metre-high steel plate levered up to block the road. The slide ended in a metalic crash as the truck drove headlong into the rust-splotched barrier.

Dvora plunged forward, her helmet cracking hard against the metal dash. Vasil clutched her by the shoulders and pulled her erect.

'Are you all right!'

She nodded, dazed by the impact. 'This barrier . . . wasn't mentioned in the briefing . . . '

A hail of bullets tore through the metal of the truck, crashed through the windows.

'Bail out!' Dvora shouted into her microphone raising her gun at the same time and putting a long burst into the doorway of a nearby building where she thought she had seen someone move. Vasil was already in the street and she dived after him. Her squad were dropping down and seeking cover, returning the fire.

'Cease firing until you see a target,' she ordered. 'Anyone hurt?'

There were cuts and bruises, no more. They had survived their first combat encounter and had all found cover, either under the truck or against the building wall.

The firing started again and slugs screamed off the road, sending up spurts of dust and fragments from the sidewalk. At the same time there was the bark of a single shot from under the truck and the firing stopped. A metallic clatter sounded, loud in the silence after the firing, as a gun fell from a window across the main road; a man's motionless arm hung down across the frame.

'There was only the one,' Grigor said, snapping the safety back on his rifle.

'We'll advance on foot,' Dvora said, looking at the map. 'But away from this main road now that the alarm is out. The alleyway across the road. Scouts out, procede as skirmishers. Go!'

The two scouts, one after another, rushed across the empty road and into the security of the alley mouth. The rest of the squad followed. They doubletimed now, aware of the quick passage of the minutes, Grigor grunting to keep up, running heavily under the thirty kilos weight of the big recoilless 50 calibre machine gun, his two ammunition carriers at his heels.

They crossed one other main avenue, in quick rushes, but met no more resistance. Steel barriers had also risen through the road's surface here; they could see more, at regular intervals, stretching away in the distance.

'One street more,' Dvora said, folding the map and putting it away. 'The building will be defended . . . ' She raised her hand and they all stopped, guns ready, alert.

A man had stepped out of a large open entrance ahead moving cautiously, his back to them. A civilian, apparently unarmed. 'Don't move and you will be all right,' Dvora said. The man turned and gasped when he saw the armed troops.

'I'm not doing nothing. I was working in there, heard the alarms, what's happening . . . '

'Back inside,' Dvora told him, signalling her squad to follow. 'What is this place?'

'Quartermaster supply. I was servicing the forklifts, charging them up.'

'Is there a way through this building?' Dvora asked?

'Yeah, sure. Stairs to the second floor, cut through the offices. Look, lady, can you tell me what's going on?'

'There has been trouble, fighting, rebel sympathisers. But we are stopping them.'

The man looked around at the silent, armed squad, their uniforms bare of identification or marks of rank. He started to ask a question, then instantly thought better of it. 'Just follow me. I'll show you the way.'

They went up one flight of stairs and started along the hall.

'You said the second floor?' Dvora was suspicious, her gun raised.

'That's right, this one. The second floor.'

She waved him on. Little details. She had forgotten that Americans called the ground floor the first. And who had forgotten the little detail about the barriers in the road? She wondered how the others were doing, but knew better than to break radio silence.

'That's the street door ahead,' their captive said 'Where you want to go.'

Dvora nodded and pointed to Grigor, who stepped forward and slapped the man on the back of the neck. He stifled the startled scream with one big hand, then eased the unconscious figure to the floor.

After unlocking the door, Dvora slowly opened it a crack and looked out, distant gunfire and explosions could be heard – then quickly closed it again. She set her radio on the command frequency.

'Black cat five to black cat one. Do you read me?'

The answer came instantly. *'Black cat five reading.'*

'In position.'

*'Black cat two is in trouble. Pinned down. You're on your own. Effect entrance now. Out.'*

The squad stood waiting for instructions, weapons ready; Dvora looked around at them. Good people. But they knew next to nothing yet about combat. They were about to learn. The survivors would be experienced.

'The groups attacking the front of the target have been held up,' she said. 'They must be meeting strong resistance. So we're going to have to do the job. The building across the road should not be as well defended. We hope. The plan is to get in there, get to the rear where it backs onto the target. We go through that wall . . . '

She broke off as they heard a siren in the street outside, growing louder. She pointed to Grigor who ran forward and dropped flat, then opened the door slightly. 'Car coming,' he said. 'It may be stopping at the doorway there – someone has come out and is waving to it.'

'We go,' Dvora said, making an instant decision. 'Bazooka. Take it out as soon as it stops. Then put one through the doorway. We'll follow right behind.'

After that it was a matter of training. Vasil rolled aside and the bazooka gunner dropped down in his spot, eyes to the sight, his weapon trained. His loader was beside him, pushing the rocket missile into the rear of the tube, slapping his shoulder to let him know it was ready. The rest of the squad moved to the sides, clear of the backlash of flame when it was fired. In the street the siren wailed down to silence as the car braked to stop.

A tongue of fire shot back from the bazooka and an explosion rocked the street outside. The loader was jamming in another rocket even as the glass from broken windows was crashing to the ground.

'Smoke, target obscured . . . ' the bazooka gunner muttered, waiting – then the flame lanced out again. The explosion, inside the building this time, was muffled. Dvora threw the door wide and led the squad in a rush.

A smoking wreck of a car, bodies burning in the crackling interior. Up the steps and through the ruined doorway, jumping over the huddle of still more bodies here. One of them alive, raising his gun, soaked in blood. Two shots cracked out and he fell with the others. They were jammed in the entrance, fighting to get in. A long hallway, running, shouting soldiers coming towards them.

'Down!' Grigor shouted, standing spread-legged while they dropped, spraying death like water from a hose from the muzzle of his machine gun. Sheets of flame blasted from the recoilless ports behind his arm, empty casings bounced clattering from the wall. The big 50 calibre slugs tore the running men apart, spun them about, hurled them down, killed them all.

There was little mopping up to do. The speed and shock of their attack had carried the defenders before it. But time was running out; they were falling behind. They moved faster now, following Dvora's directions as she consulted the detailed floor plan she had been given. Thurgood-Smythe had supplied it of course. Along with all of the other information needed to launch the attack. She had forgotten the man, and her doubts, in the cold frenzy of the fighting. Nor could she afford to think about him now.

'This is the place,' she said, when they entered the large room, one end filled with packing cases. 'That wall, where the notices are posted. Six metres in from the left hand edge.'

And they had even remembered to bring the measuring rules. Three of them had been issued so at least one would get this far. Dvora got her breath back while they made the wall.

'Take cover,' she said. 'In the hall, behind those crates. When the charges go – we go. We should be in a wide corridor leading to the entrance that has to be unblocked. This is the big one.'

Dvora checked the fuses herself; all secure. Then ran back to the hall, the wire hissing from the roller in her hand. Dropped through and hit the firing button at the same time.

For one instant as the charge blew she thought of Thurgood-Smythe, and if he had told the truth about what awaited them on the other side of the wall.

After that there was no time for thought. Coughing in the cloud of dust and smoke, scrambling through the ragged opening. Running. The surprise of the defenders as they were taken from their rear, heads turning, mouths opening even as they fell.

It was butchery. The heavy bunkers outside were open from the rear, had no defences from that flank. Grenades and gunfire cleaned them out.

'Come on now ... black cat ... the door is open ... ' she gasped into her radio. Troops appeared through the thick smoke. General Blonstein was first.

'Final goal. Missile control room,' he said. 'Follow me.'

They stopped outside the entrance to the complex, still out of breath from rushing up the three floors.

'Keep your weapons lowered when we go in there,' Blonstein said. 'We don't want any sabotage. I'll talk to them, explain, give them a story, while the rest of you filter through the control consoles. Remember, we want to capture this place, not destroy ... '

His words were interrupted by the thud of a small explosion, apparently from a room across the hall from them; a dozen gun muzzles were trained on it as the knob slowly turned. It opened even more slowly and a man appeared, leaning back against the doorjamb for support; his clothing drenched in blood.

'Thurgood-Smythe!' Dvora said.

'There has been treachery in high places,' Thurgood-Smythe whispered as he slowly slumped down to the floor.

# Chapter Twenty-Three

'They knew,' Admiral Skougaard said, staring fixedly at the identification of the enemy ships. 'They had to know. There is no other explanation for the presence of that force to be there at this time.'

'Thurgood-Smythe?' Jan said.

'You tell me.' There was no warmth or humanity left in Skougaard's voice now. 'You brought me the plan.'

'I also said that I wasn't sure if it could be trusted or not.'

'And so you did. We'll all pay with our lives for that mistake. At least we can see what is happening. I'm more sorry for the troops jammed into that transport.'

'We can still fight, can't we? We're not giving in?'

Cold anger was replaced by a wintery smile on the Admiral's face. 'We'll not give in. But I'm afraid we have no chance at all of winning. We are up against three times as many missiles as we can launch, probably more. They'll just overload our defences then come through. About all we can do is separate from the transport, fight a holding action for as long as we can in the hopes that they will survive.'

'Won't that work?'

'No. But we do it anyway. Orbital mechanics is too rigid a discipline for there to be any doubts. They will meet us, we will fight. We might injure them, probably not. They'll take us out. Then follow the transport and pick it off at their ease.'

'We can change course?'

'So can they. We cannot get away, only prolong the end.

If you have any personal messages put them through to the radio room for transmission for the second squadron to pass on . . . '

'It seems so unfair! After coming this far, after the battles for the planets, everything!'

'Since when has fairness had anything to do with winning battles? Armies and navies used to travel with priests – on both sides – each assuring the fighting men that God was on their particular side. One general said that God was on the side of the biggest battalions, which is nearer to the truth.'

There was little to add to that. Three fighting ships against one. The outcome of this encounter could not be in doubt. Under the Admiral's direction their orbits were altered slightly and the two spacers began to drift apart; there was no change in the enemy's orbit. Skougaard pointed to one of the screens.

'They are risking nothing – and leaving nothing to chance. If we hit the atmosphere at this speed we will burn up. They know we must brake, and just how much, and they will be there to meet us just when we are most vulnerable, when our speed is lowest, just outside the atmosphere.'

As the hours dragged by rage gave way to apathy; the numbness of the condemned man in his cell, waiting for the wardens. Jan thought about the road that he had followed, that had led him to this spot, at this particular time. Although he had no desire to die, he could not see how he could have done anything differently, could have followed any other path, taken any different decisions. His life was what it was, he had no regrets; other than that it was just being terminated a little earlier than he had planned.

'And now the last act begins,' Skougaard said with grim Scandinavian fatalism as sudden explosions flared in space ahead. 'They send their first missiles even though it is extreme range, knowing they can't hit us – but knowing that we have no choice, that we must expend our anti-missile defences. Attrition.'

The steady attack by the enemy missiles continued relentlessly – then stopped as suddenly as it had begun.

'Our reserves are down to twenty per cent,' Skougaard said. 'What kind of cat and mouse game are they playing at?'

'Radio contact is clear,' the operator said. 'On our frequency, but emanating from the Earth ships. They want to talk to you, Admiral.'

Skougaard hesitated a moment, then shrugged. 'Put them through.'

A communication screen flicked on with the image of a full-bearded man in full dress Space Force uniform.

'I thought it might be you, Ryzard,' the Admiral said. 'Why are you calling?'

'To offer you terms, Skougaard?'

'Surrender? I don't think I like that. You'll only kill us all in the end anyway.'

'Of course. But you'll get a few more weeks of life. A trial, a military execution.'

'Sounds charming, but not very attractive. And just what arrangements have you made for my ships to surrender?'

'Ship. Singular. They want you and your *Dannebrog* as a memorial to the failed rebellion. The other ship with you, which I assume is a troop carrier, we are blowing up. That is another kind of memorial for the rebellion.'

'You can go to hell, Ryzard, you and the rest of your murderers.'

'I thought you might say that. You always were stubborn ... '

'One question, Ryzard, a last favour for an old

198

classmate. You were informed of our plans, weren't you?'

Ryzard brushed his fingers slowly through his beard before answering. 'It can do no harm now to tell you. We knew exactly what you were going to do. You never stood a chance. Our information came right from the top . . . '

Skougaard broke the connection with a slap of his hand. 'Thurgood-Smythe. The galaxy would have been a better place if he had been smothered as an infant . . . '

A buzzer sounded stridently for attention, a red light began pulsing on one of the screens at the same time. Skougaard swung about to look at it.

'Earth-launched missiles,' he said. 'They are going to a lot of trouble to make certain of their kill. Those big ones have multiple atomic warheads. Can't be stopped by anything that we can put in front of them now. Must be a dozen of them. Launched in counter orbit, they'll be here in seconds . . . but, no! That can't be possible?'

'What?' Jan asked. 'What do you mean?'

The Admiral was struck speechless, could only point at the screen. Jan looked, seeing the plotted course of the new attack, the three enemy ships.

Distant explosions flared in space as the missiles pressed home their attack. But not at the rebels, not at all.

It was the three attacking ships that had been destroyed.

The missiles had been aimed at them, not the two rebel ships, had punched through their defences, had vaporized them utterly in the instant hell of atomic explosions.

It was unbelievable – but it had happened. In a single instant, defeat had been turned to victory. In the stunned silence that followed the Admiral's voice bellowed out clearly.

'Make a signal,' he said, an uncontrollable tremour in his voice. 'Secure for retrofiring. And prepare for landing. Enemy forces destroyed. We're going in!'

# Chapter Twenty-Four

Down out of the clear blue sky the two great spaceships fell. There was no ground control, no contract with Spaceconcent control, so they were not being guided into the landing pits. They were aimed instead for the wide stretches of concrete of the airfield. Well clear of the transport planes, they dropped down on thundering spires of flame in a crushing 5G landing. Strapped to their bunks, fighting for breath where an 80 kilo man suddenly weighed 400 kilos, the crews and the soldiers waited. As the landing legs touched the engines were cut – and they were on the ground. The reinforced concrete buckled and cracked under their weight, but the computers compensated instantly for the difference and the ships remained upright.

As the engines shut down aboard the *Dannebrog* the shields snapped away from the outside cameras and the scene appeared on every screen inside the ship. The troop carrier, with smoke still billowing up around it, suddenly changed shape as all of its cargo doors and hatches were blown out at the same instant. Landing ramps reached out and crashed down into place, while folding ladders rattled down from the open ports. The attack was on. Light tanks hurtled down the ramps and out through the smoke while soldiers swarmed like ants down the ladders. There was no sign of opposition and the attackers spread out as quickly as they could, racing towards the buildings at the edge of the field.

Admiral Skougaard was listening in on the combat

circuit. He nodded with pleasure then leaned over and switched the radio off.

'They're down and safe,' he said. 'Contact made with the Israelis and they have joined forces to knock out all of the remaining resistance. We've done our job. Now it's up to them.'

Jan watched the troops fan out through the buildings until they had vanished from sight; his thoughts going around and around and refusing to settle down. Was this it – really it? Was the war over – or would the Earth troops continue the fighting? They could not be stopped if they did; the defenders would be overrun, wiped out. But the base would be destroyed. Was the threat of this great enough to prevent the disaster?

'Here,' Skougaard said, pushing a waterglass towards Jan. 'We will drink to success now – and victory to follow soon after.'

It was akvavit not water that filled the glass and the Admiral drained his with pleasure, smacking his lips. Jan took a large swallow which was more than enough.

'Ground transportation on the way,' the radio operator said. The Admiral nodded.

'Good. We'll use the engine room lock.'

The combat car was braking to a skidding stop as they came out, the blue and white emblem of the Earth forces still marked on its side – although it was pierced by an ominous scatter of bullet holes. The Israeli driver threw the door open for them.

'They want you both at HQ,' she said, and the vehicle hurled itself forward as soon as they were inside, squealing about in a tight turn and rushing towards the exit. They bumped through the debris where an opening had been blown in the fence and on into the streets beyond. Smoking wreckage marked the scenes of the worst fighting; crumpled bodies as well. There had been losses, heaviest around the control building that had been the prime target. A field headquarters had been set up in the ground floor. They entered it by the simple expedient of walking through the gaping hole that had been blown in the outer wall. General Blonstein was talking on the radio link, but he dropped the handset when they came in and hurried over to greet them.

'We have won here,' he said. 'The last defenders have just surrendered. But there are two enemy armoured columns coming this way, as well as regiments of paratroops. We hope to have them stopped well before they arrive. Negotiations are going forward now and all the problems seem to be in hand.' He made a gesture towards the adjoining desk, at the man seated there and talking on the phone. Even from the back it was easy to recognize Thurgood-Smythe. He disconnected and turned to face them.

'Welcome back, Jan, Admiral. Things are working according to plan as you can see.' There were smears of blood on his face and his clothing was soaked and dark with even more blood.

'You've been injured,' Jan said. The corners of Thurgood-Smythe's mouth lifted slightly.

'Don't sound so hopeful, Jan. The blood is not mine. It belongs to an associate, now dead, who attempted to interfere with my plans. Auguste Blanc the director – former director I should say – of this space centre. He countermanded orders of mine to the defending fleet.'

'The ships that were waiting for us?' the Admiral said.

'Precisely. Though I really can't blame him since all of the orders I had sent out were issued in his name. In case there were difficulties I preferred the responsibility to be his, not mine. He found out what was happening and chose to go along with the ruse instead of confronting me, only countermanding my orders at the last moment. This could have been embarrassing.'

'To you,' Jan said, his voice tight with anger. 'We could have been dead.'

'But you aren't, Jan, are you? The delay was not serious in the end. Poor Auguste was fool enough to face up to me, to brag about what he had done. After taking my gun away of course. Everyone seems to have a gun these days. I tried to move away from him, but had to do it slowly in order not to startle him.' Thurgood-Smythe looked down and brushed at his blood-stained clothing. 'He was quite startled when my gun exploded. This is his blood. Stunned me a bit. Did worse to him. I was sure he would try to arrest me on his own, that is why I had the gun prepared. He was such a stupid man.'

'Mr Thurgood-Smythe enabled us to take over missile control without sabotage or damage,' General Blonstein said. 'He had the missiles fired that took out the ships that were attacking you. He is now negotiating the surrender. He has been invaluable to our cause.'

The sub machine-gun was leaning against the wall. Jan turned away, no one even noticed, and walked slowly over to it. Only when he had seized it up and swung around to face them were they aware of what he had done.

'Stand clear of him,' Jan ordered. 'I'll shoot anyone who is in the way in order to be sure that he is dead.'

The muzzle swung back and forth in a tight arc. The room was suddenly silent. There were guns on all sides, but no one was expecting this, no one was ready; they were motionless.

'Put it down, Jan,' Skougaard ordered. 'This man is on our side. Don't you understand what he has done?'

'I understand too well – not only this, but everything else that he has done. He is a liar and a murderer and he cannot be trusted. We will never know why he has done what he has done, but it doesn't matter. When he is dead we will be safe.'

Someone moved, stepping forward, and Jan swung the gun in that direction. It was Dvora.

'Jan, please,' she said. 'He is on our side. We need him . . .'

'No we don't. He wants to take over again, I am sure of that. A hero of the revolution. And when he does it will be for his own benefit. He doesn't care about us or the revolution, or anything else other than himself. There is only one way to stop him.'

'Would you shoot me as well?' she said, standing before him.

'If I had too,' he said, slowly. 'Step aside.'

She did not move – and his finger was tight on the trigger. 'Don't be a fool,' Admiral Skougaard said. 'You're dead yourself if you shoot him. Is that worth it?'

'Yes. I know what he has done. I don't want that sort of thing to ever happen again . . .'

Thurgood-Smythe walked forward and pushed Dvora to one side, coming on until he was just before the muzzle of the waiting gun.

'All right, Jan, here is your chance. Kill me and get it over with. It won't bring any of the dead back, but it will make you happy. So do it. Because if I live I might be a power in your brave new world, might even run for office in your first democratic election. That would be ironic, wouldn't it? Thurgood-Smythe, enemy of the people – saviour of the people – being elected to power by a free choice of the people. So shoot. You can't have enough faith in your new freedom to permit someone like me to live in it, can you? So you, the one who has been so much against killing, will be the first to kill in the new republic.

Why — you might even be the first one tried and condemned under the new laws.'

There was irony in his voice, but he wasn't smiling as he spoke. If he had been Jan would surely have pulled the trigger. But he didn't. It would have taken just a touch, the slightest pressure and the problem of Thurgood-Smythe would have been ended forever. But matters involving Thurgood-Smythe were never so simple.

'Tell me the truth,' Jan said, so quietly that none of the others could hear. 'Just for once in your life. Had you planned it all this way, or did you just see an opportunity to change sides and make the most of it? Which was it?'

Thurgood-Smythe looked Jan fully in the eyes as he spoke.

'My dear brother-in-law, telling you anything now would be a complete waste of time. You would not believe me whatever I said. So you will just have to make your mind up on your own for I shan't help you.'

He turned about when he had finished speaking, walked slowly away and drew out a chair and seated himself. Jan willed himself to fire. But he could not. Whatever Thurgood-Smythe had done, whatever his reasons had been, he had aided them in the end. The liberation of Earth would not have been possible without his help. With sudden insight Jan realized that the victory might have been won in another manner without Thurgood-Smythe's help; but once he had become involved the responsibility had shifted to him. All choice had been removed. Jan actually smiled as he engaged the safety with his thumb and let the gun slide to the floor.

'All right, Smitty, this round to you. You are free to go. For now. Run for office, do whatever you like. But don't forget that I am watching. Revert to your bad old ways . . .'

'I know. You will come and find me and kill me. I don't

doubt that for a second. So we will just have to let the future take care of itself, won't we.'

Suddenly Jan wanted to get out into the fresh air, to be free of this man, of the very room he was in, to forget him and the past and to look forward to the future. He was not stopped as he turned about and left. He stood outside, drawing in breath after deep breath, wondering at the emotions that tore at him. Someone was next to him; he turned and saw that it was Dvora. Without thought his arms were about her, holding her very tight.

'I am going to forget him,' Jan said in a fierce whisper. 'I'm going to put him from my mind and go home to Halvmörk, to my wife, to my people there. There's work to be done.'

'And here as well,' she said. 'And I'll go back to my husband . . . '

'You never told me,' he said, surprised, holding her at arm's length.

'You never asked.' She was smiling, brushing the hair out of her eyes, smearing even more her beautiful but battle-stained face. 'I told you that, remember? That between us, it was only chemistry. He's a rabbi, very devout and serious, but a very good pilot as well. He flew one of the planes here. I was very worried about him. The condition of the world has kept us apart too long. Now it is going to draw us together.'

Jan found himself laughing, for no reason at all, laughing until tears rolled down his face. He hugged Dvora to him then released her for the last time.

'You're right. It's over and we have to believe that it is over. And we have to work to see that it comes out right for everyone.' He looked up into the smoke-filled sky with sudden realization.

'And I'm coming back to Earth. I don't think Alzbeta will like it at first, but she will get used to it in the end.

Earth is going to be the centre of the worlds as it always has been. I can do the most for Halvmörk and its people by being right here ... '

'You can do the most for everyone. You know Earth and you know the planets and you know what people must have.'

'Freedom. They have that now. But it might be even harder to hold than it was to get.'

'It always has been,' she said. 'Read your textbooks. Most revolutions are lost after they have been won.'

'Then let us make sure that this one stays won.' He looked up at the sky again. 'I wish it were night now. I would like to see the stars.'

'They are out there. Mankind has gone out to them once and did not do very well. We have a second chance now. Let us see if we can do better this time.'

'We had better,' Jan said, thinking of the power they had, the weaponry and the infinite ways of dealing death and absolute destruction.

'We must. I doubt if we will have a third chance if we don't get it right this time.'